EDEN CROWNE

BOOK ONE

GIRL'S GUIDE
TO VOODOO BOUNTY HUNTING

Girl's Guide to Voodoo Bounty Hunting

Book 1: The Fast and the Furriest

By Eden Crowne

Copyright 2021 by Eden Crowne. All rights reserved.

ISBN: 9798840504062

Cover Art by Miblart.com

Visit Eden Crowne at: http://www.edencrowne.com

More Occult Thrillers from Eden Crowne:

Girl's Guide to Voodoo Bounty Hunting Series
Fast and the Furriest
Shifty Business
Royal Pain (coming soon!)

Dust to Dust series
Fangs for the Memories
Witch You Were Here
Ghost of a Chance

Avenging Angel Series
Fall from Grace
Perilous Grace
Deadly Grace

Fear Club Series
Cruel and Unusual Magic
Masquerade
The Summoning

Knights Divinus Mortem Series
Knight Shift

CONTENTS

Chapter One	1
Chapter Two	21
Chapter Three	41
Chapter Four	46
Chapter Five	58
Chapter Six	71
Chapter Seven	83
Chapter Eight	88
Chapter Nine	95
Chapter Ten	109

Sneak Preview: Girl's Guide to Bounty Hunting 2: Shifty Business   120

CHAPTER ONE

A toothy ten-foot electronic fish flashed fitfully in the hot morning sun. The green neon crackled as the fish opened and closed its electronic jaws. Yellow dollar signs in the fish's eyes blinked on and off in sync to some rhythm all their own. Below the fish, a billboard announced' Barracuda Bail Bonds 'in bold black letters.

Nessa looked at the address scrawled across a torn scrap of paper, then the map app on her phone, and back to the note.

Yep, this was the place.

She took off her helmet, set the kickstand on her scooter, and flipped open the top of an oversized wire basket attached to the scooter's front. A gray-striped head popped out, peering up at the blinking sign. The cat, a stocky British Shorthair, hopped to the ground.

Pim, full name Pim's Cup Whiskers Rampant, Grand Champion at the 1871 Crystal Palace Cat Show was invisible due to a rather unfortunate curse. On the Atlantic crossing from

England with Nessa's Great-Grandmother, he'd fallen for a saucy short-tailed Calico. The Calico's mistress, a Gypsy witch, had taken exception to the union and poor Pim hadn't been seen since. Except, of course, by Nessa. As her Familiar, she could see him just fine.

Looking up at the sign, he arched his back and hissed.

"I know," sighed Nessa. "What the hell, Dad?"

Dead-beat dad had skipped town leaving Barracuda Bail Bonds holding a large bond. The fact Dad owed bail money came as no surprise. That he had skipped town was also not hot news. Finding out in a phone call at seven a.m. this morning he had left her, his one and only daughter, as collateral to a supernatural Bail Bondsman a couple of blocks on the wrong side of the 91 Freeway had been a bit of a shock.

Barracuda Bail Bonds was well-known among the SoCal supernatural substrata for financial aid on a swiftly tilting scale of crimes not necessarily against the great State of California.

It quickly became apparent Dad owed a supernatural debt rather than the more mundane cash sort. After the call, Nessa had thrown some clothes and cash into a backpack, scribbled a note for her Aunt Emerald, grabbed Pim, and headed north on the Pacific Coast Highway as fast as the orange 50cc scooter could rev. They hadn't gotten very far before Dad's debt yanked her back, nearly bringing them to grief at a busy intersection in El Segundo.

The contract's supernatural tether made it clear she had no choice but to turn the scooter in the direction of Compton and the Honorable Mr. Roman Barracuda.

Nessa pulled a heavy lock and chain out of the basket and fastened the scooter to the base of the blinking neon sign. The chain had shock charms painted on each link. It was going to need them in this neighborhood.

She stood back, hands on hips, and looked at the neat one-story bungalow painted pale, sherbet yellow with white trim. Pim sat on his haunches, his long tail wrapped neatly around his front paws, and looked with her.

It was one of only a few houses left on the street. Zoning laws must have shifted seismically over the years. A used-car lot flanked the bail bonds office on one side. On the other, a furniture store that looked like it specialized in furniture that fell off trucks onto the shoulder of the 405.

She grabbed her duffel bag from the running board and slung it over her shoulder where it knocked against the faded black Old Navy backpack she always carried.

They walked up the three steps to the front porch and hesitated. A painted wooden sign was nailed at eye-level.

'Beware. Secrets will be revealed of those who cross this threshold.'

And beneath this warning, painted in a script only the magically inclined could see was added, 'Dark Spirit or Light, Betray My Trust at Your Peril.'

Pim turned right around and headed back to the scooter. Nessa considered how she could do the same. She had secrets built right into her DNA. Ones she could hardly bear the burden of knowing herself some days.

A shout of, "That door is not going to open itself!" made her jump. "Get in here young lady and bring your damn cat!"

The tether gave another yank and she gagged.

Waving Pim ahead, she tugged her sleeves over the bracelets circling both wrists and they stepped inside together.

A big black man with big black hair sat behind an oversized dark wooden desk directly opposite the door. He was wearing a lime green and gray geometric print shirt with an oversized collar. It was shiny. Seventies K.C. And the Sunshine Band shiny. He had a pair of violet-tinted granny glasses pushed halfway down his broad nose and he peered over them at her, his wide mouth turned down in a frown.

Nessa swallowed drily and looked around. The inside of the office was painted the same creamy yellow as the outside. Long rows of bleached-blond wooden blinds softened the view on the barred windows facing the street. The wooden floors were the same color as the blinds. Old-style travel posters for the Caribbean brightened the walls with splashes of pink, yellow, green, and blue. The office opened onto another room with a circular dining table, a handful of chairs, and a curtained alcove.

"You took your sweet time, Miss Scott," he said gruffly.

"Um," replied Nessa with typical articulateness.

"What's your Familiar's name?"

She was startled and didn't try to hide it. "Most people can't see him."

He looked at her over his glasses. "I am not most people."

Obviously not.

"His name is Pim, Pim's Cup Whiskers Rampant."

"Fine. So, Miss Vanessa and Mister Pim, your daddy owes me a debt which he seems to think he can run from. He cannot. You were left as collateral. As I explained on the phone several hours ago," he said the last few words with heavy emphasis.

Okay, yeah, she tried to run and then when that was denied her, stopped for gas and maybe a leisurely coffee at Coffee Bean and Tea Leaf with a fat butter croissant to share with Pim.

"Slavery is illegal," she protested.

"Not in magic," replied Barracuda clearly unimpressed. "I am collecting on your father's Bond. Do you know what I do here?"

"Kind of…" she mumbled.

Boy, she was just sparkling with conversation this morning.

"I am licensed to chase and capture those who think they are above the laws of God and man and choose to turn aside from the path of honesty. In other words, they take my money and run." He turned his head calling, "Ladies, could you join us please?"

There was a shuffle of sound from a connecting room. Nessa could see a couple of desks and rows of metal filing cabinets in what must be the back office.

Quite the largest women Nessa had ever seen emerged through the connecting doorway. They were identical twins and well over six feet tall. They looked to out-weigh their boss by a dozen pounds. Not that they were fat. Far from it.

The women were squeezed into identical black leather jumpsuits that hugged every bulging muscle and feminine curve. And their hair! Red as a tropical sunset. Tossed and teased into an up-do that added several more inches to their already impressive intimidation factor.

They were also, Nessa was certain, only marginally human.

Barracuda gestured at the women. "Meet Pansy and Rose Marie La Rue, my Bond Enforcement agents and valued partners."

They gave her surprisingly charming smiles.

Nessa automatically tried to smile back but her mouth muscles refused to respond. Gravity had inexplicably increased around her as the reality of Barracuda Bail Bonds sank in. Breathing was an effort. Her heart thudded against her chest.

One of them — Pansy or Rose Marie, she didn't know who was who — walked over and held out a hand for Pim to sniff.

Well, well. They could see him too.

"Hello there, young man," she said, her voice deep and musical with a bit of a Caribbean lilt, "aren't you just the handsomest Tom around. Yes, you are!"

Pim preened and gave the woman's hand a head butt before turning to the side and letting her stroke him.

He was a whore for a compliment.

Were these women going to chase her dad? And if they caught him, would she still be collateral?

Those were important questions. If only her tongue wasn't stuck to the roof of her mouth so she could ask.

"Skip Tracer, Bounty Hunter, or as we say here in California, Bail Recovery Enforcement Agent, whatever you choose to call it," Barracuda continued, "bond enforcement is a big part of this business. California recently made some changes in their Bail Bonds laws." He waved a hand in the air. "Not saying they weren't justified but it cut into my human bail bond business. We're focusing more on the supernatural criminal element. Since that pandemic nonsense, Infernal Courts been busier than ever. Like every day was a damn full moon."

He looked at Nessa for confirmation and she nodded automatically.

The only part she understood was the Infernal Courts. The supernatural world was not closely policed but there were rules designed to keep a lid on exactly how pervasive magic was in modern society. Extremism was the norm instead of the exception these days. Nobody wanted a return to witch hunters and bonfires.

"I keep supernatural bonds for a variety of magical tribunals and demonic agencies on the books. Pansy and Rose Marie can handle the sorry asses of the shapeshifting, bloodsucking murderers, rapists, and bank robbers who leave slime trails across my door. However, and this is a big however, we have many smaller bond clients, both human and supernatural. Recently one of my agents had an unfortunate encounter with a machete." He paused and sighed deeply. "May Raoul rest in peace."

The two large women sighed as well.

"His death left me short-handed." Smiling brightly, he gave her an expectant look. "Your daddy's bond came due just in time. Looks like your it."

"I'm *it* what?" Nessa had lost track of the conversation somewhere around the words murderers and rapists.

He grimaced. "Keep up! You, young lady, are my new supernatural skip tracer. For those low-end bond runners. Every penny counts."

"Every penny counts," echoed the twins.

"*Me?*" she said in one strangled word for what had to be obvious to the very large Mr. Roman Barracuda.

Nessa was a scrappy five-feet-two inches tall. A hundred and ten pounds on a good week when there were regular meals. She had dark brown bra-length hair and what could best be described as regular features. Few people had a chance to see the brilliant smile and deep dimples that transformed her face.

He gave her a dispassionate up and down.

"Bond Enforcement is not based on brawn alone. You have brains, or so your father says, as well as other gifts. Powerful ones."

She was going to protest but shut her mouth. He wasn't wrong. She was an Elemental, a Blood Witch with control over the air. She'd inherited it from her mother's side of the family. Among other less desirable things.

Barracuda pulled open a drawer and tossed a pair of metal handcuffs over.

"You'll need these."

She stared at the cuffs.

"And this."

He slid over a set of keys on a metal ring.

Pim jumped up onto the desk and batted the cuffs with his paw knocking them to the floor. He gave Barracuda a feline sneer, laying his ears flat.

Barracuda read the expression correctly and frowned at the cat.

Pim spun around, tail high, showing the man his butt hole. A cat version of 'Up yours!'

Barracuda rolled his eyes, "Don't you give me attitude Mr. Pim. You're what, Miss Scott? Twenty-five? Twenty-six?"

"Nineteen."

Barracuda tilted his chair away from his desk and adjusted his glasses.

One of the enormous women snorted.

Barracuda's eyes shifted to them. They suddenly got busy looking around the room like they'd never noticed those colorful travel posters before.

Their boss cleared his throat noisily and shifted through the papers on his desk. He pulled out one sheet with something paper-clipped to it and frowned.

"Never mind. In the great state of California, you can get your Bounty Hunters license at eighteen."

"No way," Nessa protested.

"I assure you, it's true."

"I can't buy alcohol but I can chase down and capture felons?"

"It's a wonderful world," he said with a grin.

"Isn't there...like...a test or something?"

He nodded. "You are absolutely right. Two separate State-administered exams. I am happy to report you did wonderfully and will have copies of the certificates to prove it."

"What about a license?"

"In California, a license is technically not necessary if you have written permission from me. Which you will. A Private Investigator's license though goes a long way."

Pulling at the paper clip, he tossed a driver's license-sized card to the woman nearest him.

"Pansy, please date that appropriately. Rose Marie, a photo if you will."

Rose Marie tugged a cellphone from her back pocket.

"Smile!" she said before clicking a picture.

"What?" said Nessa, startled.

The two women gave their boss a snappy salute and stepped into the back office.

"We will adjust it to match your Driver's License."

He held out his big hand and wriggled his fingers.

Nessa scrounged in her backpack for her wallet. She pulled the license out and handed it over. The license did indeed say Vanessa Scott, though Scott was not her real last name. She'd lost count of how many names her larcenous father had given her over the years. She used to write the new name on the underside of her wrist in Sharpie to keep up.

Since Dad had dumped her with his older sister Emerald a year ago, she'd been able to keep to Vanessa Scott. Vanessa was actually one of her names. Just not her True Name. Names had power in her world.

Barracuda got up from the desk, stepping over to the back office to hand the license to his assistants.

He returned and scooted his big chair back into place. "You also successfully completed the forty-hour police training course. And a twenty-hour insurance-approved pre-licensing class. Very diligent of you."

Nessa felt the whole situation was spiraling into farce.

"Wait, wait," her voice cracked. "I can't do this. A forty-hour class? Twenty-hours for insurance? That means there are rules. Lots and lots of rules. And procedures. Legal ones. I don't know any of them. I don't know! Please." Her voice had taken on a pleading tone, but she didn't care.

"As a supernatural Skip Tracer, there are no rules."

"What about as a human bounty hunter?" she persisted. "Cops are always around when you don't want them."

Growing up with a magical scam artist for a father, Nessa knew that only too well. The police seemed to have a sixth sense for magical mischief.

"By working for me, you are legally in pursuit of felons. There *is* paperwork and I will supply you with that before you leave here today. You must keep these papers on you at all times in case the police become involved." He gave her a squinty-eyed stare over his glasses. "Which they had better not. With the paperwork I mentioned, slightly adjusted for the magical sort, you have every right to apprehend them, even entering their home without a search warrant. The use of deadly force is frowned upon."

There was a bark of laughter from the other room.

He shifted his eyes in the direction of the laugh, "Though sometimes warranted."

There was another raucous laugh.

Pim tugged at Nessa's sleeve. He looked as puzzled as she felt.

"I'm not a detective."

Pim meowed.

"*We* are not detectives."

"No. Mr. Pim is a werecat under a rather unfortunate invisibility curse but with his own defensive arsenal. You, too, can be lethal, Miss Scott."

Nessa squirmed inwardly. How did he know all this? Pim was a werecat. A rare and deadly magical beast able to transform at will. Then she realized Dad must have told him quite a bit to convince the Bail Bondsman on the value of his daughter and Pim as collateral.

Or had Pim and her secrets revealed themselves when she crossed the threshold? She had rather a lot of secrets for someone her age.

"Do you have a car?" he said changing the subject abruptly.

"What?" The interview was going too fast; she couldn't keep up.

"An *au-to-mo-bile.*" He paused on each syllable like she was ESL or something. "A mechanical mode of transportation."

"I have a scooter."

Barracuda threw his hands up in the air. "A scooter? A damn scooter? How are you going to pursue felons, handcuff thugs and/or demons, or scrape up the remains of your quarry and bring them to judgment on a damn scooter?"

Heat was building behind her eyes, spreading down her neck and shoulders into her fingers.

God damn her father. God damn this man. God damn them all.

She jumped out of her chair and slapped her hands down on his desk. "I don't know!" she said, her voice cracking. "It was never an issue I had to consider until this moment!"

A gust of wind blew through the bungalow. It was followed swiftly by another, stronger gust.

"I don't know how to..." she pounded on his desk again causing her bracelets to spark. "How to do this! I am not my deadbeat father's keeper!"

Her eyes were burning.

"I am a college student at Santa Monica Junior College," she said. "I have a scholarship and I am going," she slapped the desk, "to go on to University as God is my witness."

Pansy and Rose Marie rewarded her with a burst of applause from the other room.

Barracuda, however, seemed unimpressed. He gave her a look she couldn't interpret, "Oh, we both know you are so much more than a college girl."

Nessa's stomach slid into her shoes.

'So much more...'

How much did he know about her?

The bad stuff? The worse stuff? The worst?

The wind flowed faster and one of the framed posters on the wall tumbled to the floor.

Nessa's hair floated up from her shoulders as a spider web of shadows spun from her fingers onto the desk.

Barracuda leaned forward, watching Nessa, eyes narrowing. Opening a drawer, he pulled out a colorful string of metal amulets.

She felt the snap and crackle of energy building across the desk. A familiar shiver of electricity sparked in her palms.

Pim yowled. His fur bristled, absorbing the rogue electricity zipping around her. His claws and fangs began to lengthen.

Pansy and Rose Marie stepped out from the backroom to stand by their boss. They did not look happy.

Roman snapped his fingers.

Around her, the floor changed. Wooden planks became a black, viscous liquid. Monstrous shapes began to ooze up from the ground.

Nessa caught her breath.

The heat behind her eyes flamed.

'*Crap, crap, crap,*" she chanted silently. She could not afford to lose another pair of contacts.

Despite the scary floor shift, she did not believe she was in danger from the Bail Bondsman. Like most of magical LA, she knew Barracuda was a Voodoo King. She also knew he followed Legba, the guardian of the crossroads between the living and spirit worlds. He stood on the side of righteousness. The profitable side of righteousness but, nevertheless, not the opposite.

She was just scared and freaking out. Freaking out was not good for Nessa or anyone nearby. Bad things happened.

Abruptly, she wrapped her hands over her chest, tucking them into her armpits. She forced herself to sit in the chair, close her eyes, and count backward from one hundred. Pim stayed where he was, a menacing growl rumbling in his throat.

'Breath in, breath out, 'she told herself.

'Breath in, breath out.'

At seventy, she opened her eyes.

The wind died with a sigh. Her hair settled around her shoulders. The snap and crackle dissipated into wherever snaps and crackles went.

Roman Barracuda's expression had changed from fierce to one of concern. He laid the amulets on the table and made a dismissing motion to Pansy and Rose Marie. With a shrug, they returned to forging her license. At least that's what Nessa assumed they were doing.

Pim had stopped his transformation. His fur was still bristling, and his ears lay flat against his head. The cat stalked over and pushed his face right up to the big man's. He angrily flicked his long tail and voiced a series of yowls, digging his claws into a sheaf of papers under his paws.

"If your Familiar is saying 'damn fool,' I agree," Barracuda said in his deep, resonant voice. "I am used to dealing with…" he paused, "individuals of a more recalcitrant nature. That was perhaps too much information delivered too forcefully."

"Ya' think?" breathed Nessa.

Pansy or her twin stepped over to hand Barracuda a laminated card and her driver's license. Pim backed up, though he stayed on the desk, the growl still rumbling.

Barracuda pushed up his glasses, carefully looking over the card front and back before handing both of them to Nessa.

Nessa had no frame of reference for Bounty Hunter or P.I. licenses. The thing looked official. State Seal, serial number, office address. Nessa groaned at the photo. And she thought the one on her driver's license was bad.

Barracuda shifted in his chair, clearing his throat. "Miss Scott, your father's debt must be paid. The Bond has been signed in blood. The contract is valid. I can neither undo nor ignore it. My hands are tied."

She looked up from the card to meet his eyes.

"Better to owe me than someone else," he said more warmly. "There are far worse collectors out there. Your father understood. It's why he came to me."

Nessa shuddered inwardly. An image of burning houses, blinding black smoke, and cries of despair flashed in her mind's eye. A man shaking her hard, ordering her to bring the lightning.

He was right. There were worse people to owe.

While Barracuda tugged some papers out from under Pim's paws, Nessa mentally tallied up her current situation.

Fact one: Today she had become an indentured servant thanks to her father.

Fact two: The bond was magical. No escape from that except death.

Fact three: The Bondholder was a Voodoo King with monsters living in his floor.

Conclusion: Her life was even more royally screwed up than before. Given her curse, how was that even possible?

He cleared his throat, sat up straight, and shifted to all-business mode. "You have some unique talents which I believe will help you adapt to this job in no time. Yours has been, shall I say, an unconventional life?"

Nessa said nothing but sniffled several times. Her nose had started to run.

"Will I..." she took a deep breath and tried to steady her voice, "will I get paid?"

Barracuda laughed loud and long.

Nessa cringed. "I have a cat to feed."

Pim had a sticky note on one back paw and was trying to vigorously shake it off. Nessa leaned over to pull it.

"Rent..." she started to add.

"You live with your Aunt Emerald in the little apartment above the garage. I know for a fact she does not charge you rent."

Not exactly. Aunt Emerald traded Nessa's help with her psychic clients for room and board.

Insert shaky voice, "I feel the spirit wind."

Cue Nessa and the wind charm.

Insert shaky voice again, "It carries the chill of the grave...."

Cue Nessa for a temperature drop.

And so on, and so forth.

"Gas?" she pursued.

Barracuda laughed again. "I will see to it that neither you, your cat, nor your transportation starves. Though we must see about finding a car for your bond enforcement work. It is difficult to transport miscreants of a supernatural nature without a back seat and a set of iron manacles bolted to the floor."

"Amen to that!" chorused the women from the back office.

Manacles?

Nessa swallowed again.

"Now," he brought his hands together and leaned forward. "When you capture your victim, I mean, um...quarry, do you know what to say?"

She looked at him blankly.

He gave an impatient sigh, "Bail Fugitive Recovery Agent. Say it."

"Bail...bail recovery..."

"Bail Fugitive Recovery Agent.

She took a shaky breath, "Bail Fugitive Recovery..."

"Agent."

"Agent. Bail Fugitive Recovery Agent."

"Be sure you announce yourself." Barracuda handed her a manila envelope. "Leave your duffel bag and get your skinny little scooter on over to the South Bay Cultural and Event Center in Torrance. You know where that is?"

Nessa nodded, clutching the envelope tightly to her chest, her hands trembling.

Okay, she had no idea. But the almighty Map App on her phone would find it.

"The details of the case are inside. This gal is not going to give you any trouble. Just bring her to the Infernal Court's regional office in Redondo Beach. The address is there," he pointed at the folder. "She's attending a meeting. Starts at noon."

"She's a witch?" asked Nessa hoarsely.

"Indeed she is. A naughty one." He shook his head making unhappy clucking sounds. "Wastin 'the time and money of her elders by missing her court date. Don't let me down, Miss Scott."

Nessa wanted to say how could she let him down when she had no idea what she was doing?

"What are you standing there for? This girl is not going to catch herself!" He shooed her off like a bug.

Nessa turned without a word and ran out of the office with Pim at her heels.

CHAPTER TWO

The South Bay Cultural and Event Center had that brutalist architecture popular in SoCal during the seventies. A gray concrete fortress where the idea of fun looked like it might be a trial by the Spanish Inquisition.

Much of Torrance felt like some sort of seventies time loop so the building fit right in.

Nessa and Pim re-locked the scooter near the event center's parking garage. Once out of the basket, Pim indicated by clawing her ankle that he had, 'things to say!'

No doubt.

Squatting, she shrugged off the backpack and took out his faded red plastic *Speak and Spell*. Cat's vocal cords – even magical cats – are not made for human speech. Pim had six claws on his front paws, the extra one working as an opposable thumb. He could read and write and type though his paws were too awkward for most keyboards. Grandma' Hattie had hit on the *Speak and Spell* back in the day. Way back. Since Nessa had inherited Pim, she and her dad had made upgrades to the machine – some highly illegal.

Pim's paws worked the simple keyboard.

"Are you out of your mind?" the female electronic voice said tonelessly.

Nessa winced. Despite the synthesizer's lack of emotion, Pim typed with attitude.

"Rock and a hard place, kitty. You felt the tether, just like me."

And he had. Pim was her Familiar, they would ghost each other's feelings 'till death do us part.'

"File. Let me see."

She put the top sheet of paper down for him to read. It included a picture of the witch, Fiona Garde. Fair-haired, blue eyes. Curses and distance spells her specialty. A Blood Witch of the Thirteen Families.

Nessa knew about them. Every witch of merit knew about *that* coven. The largest, oldest, and most powerful international organization of witches in this world and perhaps several others.

She and Pim kept reading. Legalese. Paragraph, paragraph. Council tribunal…blah, blah, blah… accused of killing a herd of sacred sheep with black magic spells for personal gain.

"Sheep?" Pim typed, the question obvious.

"Sacred sheep," affirmed Nessa.

Her cell beeped an alarm. She'd set it before leaving Barracuda's to the time of the meeting Fiona was attending.

Barracuda seemed sure the witch would be here. Maybe he placed a tracking spell on bonded clients he felt might run.

So why wasn't he tracking her father? No fool would lay out money or magic on that man without a tracking spell and possibly an iron ball and chain.

A little cluster of spidery shadows appeared at her feet much like those on Barracuda's desk. Pim sent them spinning away with the swipe of one paw and a hiss. He meowed up at her and she didn't need the *Speak and Spell* to know what he said.

Barracuda wasn't the only one with tracking spells.

Nessa asked at the reception desk where the DMA (Dark Magic Anonymous) meeting was being held. She followed the directions downstairs. They were in the Sequoia Room; the second basement. She took her time checking the layout of the entire basement floor before cautiously opening the door.

A dozen or so men and women and one person in a blue furry wolf costume were sitting in a circle on folding metal chairs. Most were looking attentively at a handsome red-headed woman in a blue-print wrap dress standing at a podium.

The meeting had already begun. With a shy wave at the assembled group, Nessa quietly took the nearest empty seat in the circle.

"My name is Phoebe and I am a Dark Magic addict," said the woman at the podium.

"Hello, Phoebe," chorused the group.

"Up yours, Phoebe," the woman next to Nessa mumbled under her breath.

The furry wolf said nothing.

Nessa glanced at the young woman in the chair and almost laughed. Short blond hair cut in a fashionable bob, green eyes, Gucci sunglasses pushing back her side-swept bangs. She'd sat right next to Fiona What's-Her-Name from Barracuda's file. What were the odds?

There was another empty chair on the woman's other side. Hmmm.

Perhaps Fiona was not a popular member of the DMA.

Pim jumped out of Nessa's arms to stalk around their quarry. No one could see him, she was sure, even in this gathering. His curse was pretty much all-encompassing –except when crossing the threshold of a Voodoo King it appeared.

Despite Fiona's presence, her file indicated she was not at all interested in giving up Dark Magic. If her Coven Tribunal had not ordered her to attend these meetings, she would probably be figuring out how to hex them all.

Nessa glanced curiously at the fuzzy wolf.

Not fuzzy.

Furry.

That's it. He was a Furry. One of those cos-playing sub-tribes who dressed as anthropomorphic animals to feel social. She'd heard it was also a kinky sex thing with a subculture of the subculture. Furry porn.

'Freaks,' she thought. Then mentally slapped herself. She ran around with an invisible werecat and could command the wind with a snap of her fingers. Who was she to call anyone a freak?

Furries came in all sorts of incarnations: dogs, cats, wolves, foxes, bears, lions, even dragons. To do this they made, purchased, or rented Furry suits or costumes or whatever they called them. A good one could cost thousands of dollars. Wolf-guy's suit had to be top-of-the-line. She watched him flex his finger-paws. It looked as though the muscles in his furry arms bunched to match. Nessa was torn between ridicule and admiration for his attention to detail.

As if sensing her gaze, he turned his face in her direction and arched his brows. The wolf's mouth opened in a wicked grin. Maybe it was just the costume's expression but Nessa felt like a double-decker bacon sandwich at a free lunch for pig farmers.

Its big eyes blinked.

Whoa! Too much realism.

Pim tapped her ankle and she shifted her gaze. He gave her a 'Now what?' look.

Good question.

With a gurgle, her stomach slid about six inches toward her knees. She couldn't just jump up and yell… what was she supposed to say? Bond…um… bond…agent...enforcement. No. Damn it.

She googled "California Bail Bond Agent" on her cell. Blah, blah, blah. Ah! Bail Fugitive Recovery Agent.

Right. Yell that and then handcuff witchy-witch.

Okay. Realistically, that was not happening. She'd wait until the meeting ended. Barracuda said the girl wouldn't give her any trouble.

Nessa stole another glance at the pretty blonde. She was wearing a light turquoise argyle twin set and short pink pleated skirt. Her long legs were crossed. She was swinging one Tory Birch pink ballet flat impatiently, her features twisted into a bored frown. She'd probably had the shoes dyed to match the skirt.

Nessa was not sure about Barracuda's assessment. This girl looked like plenty of trouble.

Pim jumped into her lap and she began stroking his back nervously.

This earned her a WTF look from the girl.

That happened a lot. She could see Pim clearly and kept forgetting to everyone else, she looked like some crazy girl petting her imaginary unicorn.

Phoebe babbled on and on about a spell involving the Palos Verde PTA president or something.

A couple of chairs away sat a slim, good-looking guy, brown skin, black hair with a natural wave brushed back from his forehead. Latino maybe?

Those cheekbones!

East Indian?

A bit of a mix, she decided.

He was wearing summer wool slacks in a slate gray, a deceptively simple white tee, and a deconstructed black jacket. His black loafers had to be hand sewn. Her dad might have been a scam artist but he taught her, in addition to survival skills, how to evaluate good clothes. After all, the richer the mark, the bigger the take.

His eyes drifted lazily across the room to meet hers. Chocolate brown with pupils the size of nickels. He didn't smile but his knife-cut lips twitched ever so slightly at the corners.

This guy looked like someone who understood how to benefit from some carefully placed dark magic. Probably why he was here.

Phoebe finally wound up her story about the Palos Verde PTA and flesh-eating bacteria. Did she say she'd cursed the President and she died or did she say 'almost died'? Who knew the PTA in the South Bay was so cutthroat?

Nessa automatically analyzed the woman's clothes from the ground up as she walked by. Fake Jimmy Choos. The buckles were wrong. And she'd bet Pim's catnip the blue Dianne von Furstenberg wrap dress was a knock-off from that place in Glendale on Brand. How much of a dark magic threat could she be if she was wearing knock-offs?

The woman sat down and a tall man with salt and pepper hair and a soul patch goatee pointed a finger in Fiona's direction. Group coordinator maybe?

The blond stood, groaned, and walked with a becoming sway of her narrow hips to the podium.

Tossing her hair, she said, "My name is Fiona and I, too, am a Dark Magic addict. Unlike Phoebe, I am not interested in giving it up. I killed a bunch of sheep in Topanga Canyon by mistake. So what? If my Coven Master Margaret *holier-than-thou* Halloran had not laid a Geas on me to attend these stupid meetings, I would be hitting Frieda's in the Americana with a glass of bubbly at my lips and salsa on my chin."

'Called it!' Nessa thought to herself.

"Perhaps why your coven Master asked you to come?" prompted Salt-and-Pepper Hair.

"Well, there was this house," said Fiona. "I was working a spell to get the price down. Seemed to me like a perfectly valid reason to toss a few hexes."

"I'm sure that wasn't all," he started to say. "The sheep..."

An older woman with gray hair interrupted, "Sheep, smeep. Where's the house?"

"Glendale," said Fiona. "Walking distance to the Whole Foods on Brand *and* Trader Joe's," she smirked.

Walking distance to two supermarkets? Fiona had the right to smirk.

"Shit," said one of the men, red hair and freckles, heavyset, thick glasses, Dodger's cap. "That's near the entrance to the 134 and not far from the 5."

"Plus you can take Brand all the way to the 101," added the gray-haired women. "Surface streets are so much better at rush hour."

Commuting and beating traffic were the fundamental concerns of LA life. Much more important than Dark Magic confessions.

"How many bedrooms," asked Salt-and-Pepper Hair.

Fiona smiled, "Two bedrooms, two baths, and half bath for guests. Carport, new fixtures, and appliances."

The guy in the Dodger's cap leaned forward eagerly, hands clenched. "How much?"

Fiona told them how much she paid versus the original asking price.

The woman with gray hair whistled, "I'd kill more than a few sheep for that."

Salt-and-Pepper Hair's expression said he would too, but he moved his hands in a damping down gesture trying to reassert his role as moderator. They were here, after all, to stop using Dark Magic for fun and profit.

And that's when things got interesting.

Furry Wolf jumped to his feet. He was holding something shiny in one paw.

Good-Looking Guy pulled a gun and fired.

Everyone started screaming and Nessa mentally cursed her deadbeat dad *again*.

She was on her feet and running for Fiona before Good-Looking Guy had even gotten off his shot. She'd noticed the shift in Furry Wolf's body language. The sudden tension in his legs, the alert set of his head.

So many flashbacks to life with Dad.

She plowed into the podium taking it and Fiona down. The sharp object flew over Nessa's shoulder and embedded itself quivering in the wall.

The shot brought Furry Wolf to its knees.

Nessa grabbed Fiona's arm and pulled her toward the door, Pim in the lead.

Fiona held back a little until Nessa said, "It's after you!"

No more urging was needed. As they barreled through the double doors, another gunshot barked behind them.

Pim skidded to a stop by Nessa, sending Fiona sprawling as she tripped over the invisible cat.

They needed to block the door. Jam the handle and lock furry-guy inside. Nessa had spied the firehose case and extinguisher near the stairs on the way in. Deadbeat Dad had thoroughly drilled into her the need to locate escape routes and possible weapons. She did it automatically.

The door was thrown open, knocking Fiona back to her knees as she tried to pick herself up.

"Fuck!" Fiona yelled, hitting the floor with a *thump*.

Nessa spun around to see the guy in nice slacks, gun still in hand, turn and fire two more rounds. The screams from the

Sequoia room increased in volume. He shoved the doors closed and backed up against them bracing his feet.

There was a crash as someone hit the door from the other side.

Nessa smashed the glass case with her elbow and grabbed the hose on the metal reel. She pulled it out.

And out, and out. How long was this damn hose?

The guy was shoved a few inches forward and a furry hand grabbed the edge of one door. Pim jumped and took a vicious bite of the hand. The Furry howled and the hand disappeared.

Good-Looking Guy grabbed the hose, back still against the door. The two of them threaded part of the canvas through the handles and pulled it tight. The guy had more strength than her and he knotted it. There was a furious pounding from the other side.

Dark Magic Anonymous had one of the free community rooms in the far corner of the second basement. Nessa didn't wait to see if the hose would hold. She yanked Fiona to her feet and ran in the direction of the main stairs.

Pim bounded ahead, transforming in seconds. He was completely visible in his werecat form and Fiona squealed at his sudden appearance. The werecat was a nightmarish version of the plump grey and white striped kitty: bigger than a full-grown lynx with scythe-like teeth and claws, his stripes squished together in a muddy mix.

Misjudging a jump, he smacked into the railing.

Sadly, his curse bled ever so slightly into his alter ego creating a bit of a depth perception problem. Glasses would probably help but a reliable way to keep glasses on in this alternate form had so far eluded them.

On the landing of the first basement stairs, Pim yowled a war cry. A second ferocious howl answered from above.

Crap, there were more.

Pim launched himself up the stairs.

Furious yowls and howls and the smack of bodies echoed down the stairwell. Nessa held Fiona back and crouched low on the step.

"What did you do," she panted at Fiona, "to those sheep?"

Fiona waved her hand, "Oh that. Like I said, about the house. I needed two things." She counted off on her fingers. "One, for the price to come down. Two, to remove the person in front of me in the buying queue. The houses on either side sort of burned down along with the trees in the house I wanted. Front *and* back yard. Bang! Price drop. Then the buyer in front of me almost drowned."

Nessa gave her an appropriately appalled look.

"In a bathtub, okay? He didn't die. And it's just a little coma. He's blinking his eyes now and everything. His stupid wife broke her own legs when she slipped on the bathwater. Clumsy idiot and so not my fault, as I told the Coven Tribunal. But I got the house," she said triumphantly. "And so what if I worked a spell? I was tired of renting. Unfortunately, I had to off-load a shitload of Dark Magic. You know, making sure it wouldn't come back to bite me in the ass."

Nessa understood only too well. What goes around comes around in magic - unless you re-route the energy onto someone or something else. No need to blacken your soul unnecessarily. Except, magic had a way of sneaking around the corner and knocking you flat anyway.

Nessa's mother had learned that lesson too late.

"I didn't realize the backwash from those spells would require quite that much chaos," continued Fiona, obviously unrepentant. "The Council pointed out in addition to the sheep I caused a landslide in Topanga Canyon. The road was blocked for days. I, in turn, said they could hardly blame me for infrastructure flaws by the California Department of Highways."

The howls above them grew louder. Nessa's skin began to itch and a gust of wind swirled up the stairwell.

"They weren't just any sheep," said Good-Looking Guy, "they were sacred Navajo sheep."

"In Topanga *freaking* canyon!" snapped Fiona. "Navajo live in Arizona."

"Seems not all of them," said the guy.

"And what's it to you, anyway?" she demanded.

Nessa began to edge her way up the stairs, the sounds of battle receding a little.

She heard the guy say, "I represent the Council of Thirteen Families. We work in league with the Infernal Courts."

"You're here for me?" squeaked Fiona, pushing up against Nessa.

Nessa shrugged her back. "Get in line, dude. I am here for her! Roman Barracuda sent me."

"Not her," said the guy, "the assassins. The Shaman who cared for the sheep expected the Tribunal would let you off with a slap on the wrist and he was out for blood. My superiors felt he was going to call a vendetta on you. An unlicensed one. I came here expecting an attack."

"By Furries?" asked Nessa.

He looked up at her with a rueful smile, "No, I will admit that was a surprise."

"*Sheep*!" said Fiona meaningfully, "They were just sheep! It's not that big a crime."

"It was to the Shaman," he said.

Nessa ignored the sheep. "So you're a cop?"

He drew his brows together in a frown line. "Well, sort of, I guess."

"Do you have a badge," demanded Nessa.

"Yeah."

Nessa thrust out her hand and made a 'give it here' gesture. "Let me see some I.D. Because I don't know if I believe you."

With a look like he was humoring her, the guy pulled out a small brown leather billfold and flipped it open. There was a California PI license and another metal badge inscribed in, she looked closer, Latin.

Nessa's Latin was limited to her Grandmother's spells she'd memorized and Caesar's *Vene Vidi Vinci*. Deadbeat Dad's favorite thing to say after a successful scam: I came, I saw, I conquered.

"Is it real? Because those are easy to fake." She should know. Barracuda just made one for her.

"Of course it's real." He put it back in his pants pocket.

"So you're a Witch Cop."

"I am not a Witch Cop," he protested.

"You have a badge, you're a witch, and you shot the blue Furry. You are so definitely a Witch Cop."

Fiona made a sound of exasperation. "Are you here to protect me?"

"Nope. Here to bring justice if they *succeeded* in killing you. I didn't really expect you to get out of the way." He pointed with his chin at Nessa. "You're fast. The Furry had a poison hex on a knife ready to go when you tackled the sheep-killer and hightailed it out of the room. I went ahead and shot him anyway. Intent is almost as good as after the fact."

"Didn't help," Nessa scoffed.

"Yeah, kind of thought that hollow point would at least slow it down."

"Who cares. Why is Barracuda after me?" Fiona demanded.

"Keep your voice down!" Nessa hissed. "Bond or bail thing. You missed some kind of witchy trial date."

"That's next week!" Fiona protested shrilly.

"*Shhh!* Monday. The tribunal stuff was Monday. Today is Wednesday."

The girl's jaw fell. "You are shitting me." She grabbed her phone, tapping at the screen.

It had gone quiet up above. Encouraged by the silence, Nessa edged cautiously up the next set of stairs. A green Furry tiger costume was sprawled on the upper landing. Pim straddled it, his mouth around the tiger's throat.

The Furry lay unmoving, paws held stiffly in front. Nessa could see the black spells circling each, ready to throw.

Nessa moved closer. Pim snarled, his jaw closing slightly on its throat. He was waiting for Nessa's orders. Even with his bad eyesight, he could smell it was her.

Nessa stared at the deep gouges and bloody tears on the tiger's arms and chest and across one side of its face.

She could clearly see the fur was attached to skin and the skin was part of a body. A body of flesh and blood.

The Furry tiger was not a costume at all.

"What the hell?" she said out loud.

Shifters, despite what movies would have you believe, are not common. The energy needed to transform from human to animal is enormous and often fatal after a few years. Most true Were creatures were already animals, like Pim. Magical ones that most assumed originated in the Fae lands. Or maybe Hell.

The magical transformation was built into their DNA. Effortless. As if they just switched places in time and space. The

Werewolves she'd met had been Lobo or Loba, wolves that could shift into people. Not the other way around.

But how could a costume come to life?

Fiona pushed closer. "Fuck me!"

She raised her phone.

"Are you taking pictures?" Nessa demanded.

"It's an Instagram moment," she replied, nonchalantly clicking away.

"Evidence, idiot," snapped Nessa, shoving the phone down.

Fiona did an eye roll to express her 'so don't care' feelings.

Good-Looking Guy had his gun out. "Why isn't he moving? He's not dead, I can see him breathing."

"Poison," Nessa answered curtly, shrugging out of her backpack and zipping it open.

Magical evolution had made up for Pim's smaller size by giving the werecat a secret weapon. Both hind legs had poison sacks with a small extendable claw that injected paralyzing nerve toxin into his attacker. It wouldn't kill but did render them powerless for a time.

She pulled out a bottle of water and a bag of salt. Nessa never went anywhere without a bag of sea salt.

She poured a hefty amount of salt into the water and gave it a vigorous shake. Twisting off the cap she splashed it over the Furry's paws. The toxin had strangled its voice but the creature gave a hissing moan as the saltwater burned away the magic spells he held.

Throwing the salt and water back in the backpack, she took the handcuffs out of her pocket and held them out to Good-Looking Guy.

"What?" he said blankly.

Nessa rolled her eyes, "Cuff his hand to the railing. Pim," she ordered, "let him go."

Good-Looking Guy seemed reluctant to touch the tiger and she couldn't blame him. Weird vibes were coming off this thing.

She leaned over and strained to shove the tiger closer to the railing. Between them, with no help from Fiona, they got his wrists cuffed around the metal. Nessa took the left wrist; Good-Looking Guy the right.

"Why don't you just kill it?" Fiona asked in a bored voice and waving a hand negligently in the Furry's direction.

"A dead body means cops," explained Nessa. "Crime Scene guys. Evidence. Like your stupid photos. Evidence is bad. This way, only the Furry explains how it got chained to the railing. Kind of doubt our names will come up."

The tiger had a lot of mass. Pim's poison might not hold much longer.

A loud crash accompanied by an unearthly howl echoed from the second basement.

Furry Number One must have gotten through the door.

Time to go.

Nessa was already moving up the stairs.

At the first basement landing, she hesitated, then skipped ahead a few steps, looked around the bend and up to the main floor.

Several figures at the next landing stared back. A dog, a cat, a bear. Furries.

Fiona and the guy peeked over her shoulder.

"How many of these bastards are there?" said Fiona.

"Those must have been some really terrific sheep," Nessa muttered.

This floor should mirror the one underneath. That meant there was an emergency exit onto the fire stairs at the end of the first basement corridor.

"Come on," she said, pushing past them and down the uniformly beige hallway, her footsteps muffled on the industrial-grade carpeting. "Pim can't handle three. We'll try the fire exit."

"Who's Pim," shouted Fiona, running after Nessa.

"My cat," she said over her shoulder, pointing at the werecat.

The itching escalated unbearably on Nessa's skin as she pulled energy from the air. Little electrical shocks zipped up and down her spine, working their way through her shoulders and into her hands. She didn't fight them.

A gust of wind rushed ahead, ripping papers from a bulletin board and tossing a stack of pamphlets off a side table.

Pim abruptly stopped and spun around, ears flattened to his head. His lips curled back over his fangs.

Fiona and the guy ran for the fire door but Nessa stopped with Pim.

Blue Wolf stepped onto the landing.

Nessa reached to her waist and ran a thumb over one of the silver charms on her summoning belt. Heat sparked into her hand. She mentally blew on the embers of that fire, letting them flare.

Extending her left hand, she moved her thumb to the next charm on the belt, an embroidered sigil. With an incantation that seared her lips as she spoke, she summoned the wind.

Air *whooshed* back along the hallway, a whirling dervish that circled wildly around her and Pim. They braced themselves against the pull of Elemental energy.

Blue Wolf came straight at her, teeth bared. He ran on two legs but moved with the feral grace and power of a wild animal.

The Wolf was so close she could see his nostrils flare. Nessa breathed in deeply. She held the air for a heartbeat, then whistled it out.

At the same time, she raised her arms and brought her bracelets together with a swift hard motion. They were not gold or silver or brass. They were inlaid with flint. Once, twice, and a spark.

She spoke the true name of the lightning and with the spark, ignited the chaotic energy circling her.

The lightning strike hit with an explosive *crack*, flinging the beast up to the ceiling in a blinding flash of light. He smashed into the dated acoustic tile panels. A dozen cracked and fell to the floor. The whirlwind grabbed hold as the Wolf fell, just as she told it to, hurtling him back to the main stairwell and out of sight.

A couple of sprinklers in the ceiling started to spray water. Nessa knew from her dad that a burst of heat did not automatically set off the entire fire prevention system in a building.

Nessa ran to the emergency exit and pushed through with Pim.

The others were already two flights up.

"Thanks for waiting, jerks!" she shouted, taking the metal stairs two at a time.

Their lead hadn't done them much good.

Fiona was pushing frantically against the handle of the emergency door to the first floor. "Open, damn it!" she shouted.

Banging hard with both fists, the guy yelled, "Help! Open the door!"

"What about the door outside?" She pushed at the emergency door opposite to no effect.

"Locked," said the guy.

"That's a fire code violation," Fiona said indignantly.

Nessa heard raised voices from the other side of the hallway door, sounds of an argument. Abruptly, the door swung open.

A couple of Furries, a brown and white Beagle and a Tabby Cat, stood in the doorway.

"Gotcha'!" they shouted.

CHAPTER THREE

Good-Looking Guy tackled the dog.

Nessa and Pim went for the Tabby, hitting it high and low.

Pim plunged his front claws into the Furry's calf, biting hard on the thigh. Nessa elbowed Tabby in the face with one arm and grabbed the police baton clipped to the back of her jeans with the other. Snapping it out, she whacked the cat on the chest.

Nessa was small, she needed an advantage against larger opponents. Much like Pim's poison claws, Nessa's baton gave her an edge. She'd seen Lucy Lu use it on reruns of *Elementary* and knew it was the weapon for her. Plus, the baton was non-lethal. She meant what she said to Fiona. Bodies and police were to be avoided at all costs. Yet another life lesson from Daddy Dearest.

With a throaty gurgle and what sounded like a yelp, the Tabby went down.

Down did not mean out, from her experience. Nessa smacked it on the head with her baton.

"Ow, ow, ow," came a muffled voice, "Cut it out! God! Please!"

Nessa paused.

Tabby's mouth wasn't moving. That voice came from inside the Furry.

'Oh crap, 'Nessa thought.

She slipped her hand quickly inside the baton strap and let it hang. Placing her palms on either side of the Tabby's head, she twisted. The cat head popped off revealing a sweating young man with a mass of brown curls and a bloody nose.

"Stop hitting me!" he shouted shrilly and started to cry.

Good-Looking Guy was in the process of strangling the dog. He paused and met her eyes. Without a word, he shifted his hands and pulled. The head came off easily revealing a plump-faced girl, her blue-dyed hair pulled in a ponytail.

She started to scream.

Pim, who was still in his werecat form, stepped forward menacingly and the girl stopped screaming and fell back, eyes closed, mouth slack.

"Did she just faint?" Nessa asked.

The guy gave the dog costume a shake. Her head lolled limply.

"Looks like it."

A movement a few feet away made them look.

Two more Furries, another dog– this one pink -- and an orange monkey stood side by side, staring.

"Boo!" yelled Good-Looking Guy.

With a strangled, "*Eep!*" they turned and ran in the other direction.

Nessa pulled together the chaotic energy still zipping around her body. With a word, she shaped it into a sparking, spitting ball of electricity.

"You know what they are, don't you!" she demanded, shoving the ball in Good-Looking Guy's face. "Not these," she indicated the Tabby, who was still crying, and the Beagle, still not moving. "The others."

He flinched at the hot sparks. "They're Skinwalkers that's the only thing they could be."

Nessa snorted, "No they're not. Skinwalkers transform into real animals. It's Navajo black magic."

"Not just Navajo," the guy said.

"This is freaking Torrance!" squealed Fiona. "How did they even get here?"

Good-Looking Guy made a face. "Your shaman must have cashed in his Southwest Frequent Flyer miles."

"Whatever," growled Nessa. "Skinwalkers need the skin of the animal they change into as part of the process. There are no real green tigers and blue wolves."

The guy shrugged dramatically, "They aren't demons."

"How do you know?"

He pulled a string of crystal talismans out from his T-shirt. "This would tell me. And they're not werebeasts either. I think that's clear. That leaves Skinwalkers."

"I bet they murder the owner of the costume," said Fiona, touching up her blush with a brush from a sleek black and gold compact she'd pulled from her bag. "Take part of their skin and blood, then some skin and blood of the animal the costume represents. They fuse all of it *with* the costume to initiate the transformation process."

Nessa and Good-Looking Guy stared at her.

"*What?*" she demanded irritably. "I know things, too!"

"Why?" said Nessa.

"Why do I know things? Remember I did hex the price of a two-bedroom house in Glendale down by a fourth."

Nessa rolled her eyes, "No. Why would Navajo Skinwalkers want to turn into Furries?"

Good-Looking Guy gave the two fuzzy beasts a speculative once over. "Expanding horizons, maybe? Can't exactly run around in coyote or cougar form in the street in daylight. You'll get shot. The Furry cover lets them move around with people just thinking they're weird. Plus, they can drive."

Nessa released a pinch of energy at Mr. Witch Cop making him gasp. " You knew they were going to be here?"

"Cut that out!" he protested, pushing her away. "No. I expected thuggish hitmen. I mean it was Topanga Canyon for Christ's sake."

"Right?" seconded Fiona.

"And these guys?" She waved her other hand at the two figures on the ground." They are not Skinwalkers. Why were they waiting for us?"

"No clue."

"Screw this," declared Fiona, shoving the compact back in her bag.

It was a vintage Gucci, Nessa noticed with painful pangs of envy.

"I am so out of here."

And damn if the witch didn't walk away.

Nessa had a feeling she would not get far.

CHAPTER FOUR

"Stop crying," she said roughly to the man-child in the cat costume. "You're not hurt."

He looked very much like he wished to disagree.

"Why were you blocking the door? Because I think that's totally what you were doing."

"Yeah," jumped in Good-Looking Guy a little belatedly. "Why were you blocking the door?"

Nessa shook a finger at him. "Shouldn't you be off chasing the Skinwalkers? *Mr. Witch Cop.*" She put imaginary quotation marks around the words with one hand.

"They are going to come to you and Fiona. I can wait." He shrugged. "Easy peasie."

Easy peasie? Nessa looked at him more closely.

The hip sophistication of the clothes and good haircut had been misleading. He couldn't be more than a couple of years older than her.

Good-Looking Guy pulled Tabby to his feet.

'Talk," he said giving him a shake. "You were at the door because?"

"It's a game," Tabby whined, sniffling loudly. He was going to start crying again, Nessa was sure.

"A game?" said Good-Looking Guy. "And you're just people?"

"Of course we're people. What are you? High?" His voice broke and he began to sob.

Good-Looking Guy made a show of pulling out his gun. "Why are you chasing us?"

"A party game," Tabby said in a rush. "We were told she," he pointed in the direction Fiona had gone, "was the quarry and we were to try and catch her. It was going to be filmed, they said. Cat and Mouse. Fun."

Pim hissed a series of meows Nessa interpreted as, "Oh good grief."

"And nobody thought this was weird?" Nessa asked.

Man-child in the Tabby costume put both paws up in a shrug.

Right, Nessa thought. Asking someone who prances around in public dressed in a furry anthropomorphic animal costume to define weird was borderline pointless.

"So is this a Flash Mob thing?" Good-Looking Guy asked.

Tabby looked confused. "What do you mean?'

"There are a bunch of you galloping around the center. Are the people who run this place okay with that?"

"Well, yeah. It's the convention."

Convention? Nessa did not like the sound of that. She grabbed the Tabby head and snapped her baton back in place.

"Show us." She shoved him in the direction the pink wolf and the monkey had taken.

Fiona came running back to them as fast as her Tory Burch flats could take her.

"Guys," she said breathlessly, "at the front door. Native American-ish muscle."

Native American-ish? What did that even mean? But Nessa had been right. The front door was not going to be an easy exit. The Skinwalkers had human reinforcements. They needed another way out.

Out of the corner of her eye, she saw Good-Looking Guy pick up the Beagle head.

Tabby Cat led them in a different direction than Fiona had run. The drab side corridor very soon turned into a wide carpeted hallway with hanging light fixtures instead of the industrial-fuggly fluorescent lights in the rest of the building. This must be the entrance to the ballroom. Several sets of double doors lined the hallway but only one was open. Next to the entrance stood a large poster mounted on an easel declaring'"LA Furry Society Third Anniversary Gala.'

Oh. Great. Everyone in costume could be playing the game. Chasing Fiona.

Fiona looked at Nessa and for the first time, the danger of their situation seemed to hit her.

"We are so fucked," she moaned.

"Who you calling *we*, sister?" Nessa snapped.

Nessa was not going to throw herself under the bus for this self-indulgent witch. If it came to Fiona or her, Nessa knew who she was choosing.

Good-Looking Guy grabbed the Tabby by the shoulders and spun him around. "You must have a Furry group chat, tell them to stop the game."

He shook his head, "I can't. We left our phones with the organizers. That was one of the rules. We're supposed to use our animal senses."

Fiona snorted derisively.

Nessa put on the Tabby head, "Safety in numbers. We're going in. There's sure to be another exit."

Good-Looking Guy popped on the Beagle head as they walked to the reception desk just inside the door.

"Tickets?" said a chirpy female voice in a curvy fox costume.

A fox with breasts.

It was such a Pixar moment.

Nessa shoved the guy in the Furry costume forward.

"They're with me." He pulled a lanyard around his neck from inside his costume and showed the card to the fox.

Nessa and Good-Looking Guy started inside.

Pim hesitated at the threshold even as Nessa but a foot over the entrance.

The official entrance.

He yowled a warning.

Too late. She felt the magic crawl up her foot, to her hips, and into her heart.

She gasped.

'Stupid, stupid girl,' she cursed silently.

The Skinwalkers had placed some sort of revealing spell on the threshold. They knew Fiona was a witch. In case she escaped their first attempt, they must have thought she might try to disguise herself with a *Glamour* and get lost in the crowd.

But they'd caught someone else hiding in a shadow spell.

Nessa.

Pim, hissing, his back arched, gamely moved to follow his mistress.

The Fox said "Eek!" and jumped out of her chair at the sight of Pim. Granted he looked like a long-tailed hell beast from your worst nightmare, so maybe the 'eek' was justified.

"What is that!" she squealed.

"It's my cat. Cool costume, right?" Nessa replied without skipping a beat.

Pim jumped with a howl, turning a sideways somersault as the threshold magic hit him.

Fox Girl said "Eek!" again.

Nessa leaned over to run a hand along his back, "I'm sorry," she whispered. "I have screwed up royally."

"Ticket?" Fox girl asked Fiona in a strangled voice.

"Fuck off!" snarled the witch following them inside.

They passed through a short tunnel of streamers and balloons, past a line of luxurious Instagram photo stations with castle, jungle, or mountain scenes, and into the ballroom.

Nessa's skin prickled, the hair rising along her arms and the back of her neck as they walked by the photo stands. She looked down at Pim.

His hair was starting to stand on end as well.

She felt a little snap and crackle in her fingertips.

Weird. This wasn't part of the threshold spell.

They entered the ballroom. Here, rows of vendors and food and drink stations were set up in a large circle; tables and chairs in the center. A stage stood at the opposite end. The room smelled like churros and beer and was filled with music, conversation, and Furries.

Lots and lots of Furries.

Dog people. Cat people. Bird people. Two-legged dragon people.

Two hundred? Three hundred?

The explanation for the snap and crackle now became abundantly clear.

Static electricity.

All this polyester fur rubbing together was storing an impressive imbalance of negative and positive charged particles looking for release. As an Air Elemental, Nessa was in tune with the atmosphere and the air here was electric. Literally.

Pim sneezed again and the fur around his neck puffed out in a ball, almost obscuring his eyes.

At least she had more room to fight. Though fighting might not be a good idea. Elemental magic had a wild side. Small and focused it was not. A lightning storm or tornado could take out more than the Skinwalkers.

She stole a glance at Good-Looking Guy. His Council might send him after *her* if that happened. Deadbeat Dad had been extremely careful not to incur either the interest or the wrath of the Thirteen Families.

Nessa craned her neck to see over the Furries. There would be emergency exits from the ballroom. Legally there had to be.

Standing on tip-toe she spied a set of doors on the far wall, to the right and back.

Nessa squatted in front of the werecat. "Pim, can you tell who is a Furry and who is a Skinwalker?"

Pim gave her an off-balance nod. The zap from the threshold spell looked like it might have scrambled his nervous system a little. Not difficult to do in this form. Were-Pim was always slightly wonky.

She put her hands on either side of his face. "Change back, kitty. Okay?"

It took a few moments for her words to sink in. He shuddered. His fur rippled. With a quiet *pop*, the stocky English Shorthair was back. Another *pop* and his hair poofed out like a cartoon kitty who had stuck its claw in a light socket.

His ears and tail drooped. He looked as tired as Nessa felt. Magic takes energy and their batteries were running low.

Fiona flipped around, phone high, and smiled expertly for a selfie. One of several.

"What do you think you're doing" Nessa hissed, jumping to her feet and batting at the phone.

Fiona was taller than her and she held it out of reach. "Selfies with the freaks, it's Insta-perfect."

And damn if she didn't fake smile for another picture.

She pulled Good-Looking Guy in with her. "Come on Witch Cop, smile."

He leaned in and winked expertly.

They made peace signs.

Nessa threw her hands in the air. "You are both idiots."

That's when she saw Man-Child in the Tabby costume snapping pictures of all of them.

"Give me that!"

She snatched the phone out of his hands and deleted the photos that showed her. Nessa stayed off all Social Media. She had to.

Nessa shoved the phone back. "You! Find the moderator or whoever is in charge and make an announcement over the audio system that this stupid hide and seek game is over. The admin here at the center has insisted and everyone should return for their phones or something. Do that and I will give you back your cat head," she leaned close trying to look menacing. "Don't do it and I will come for yours."

The guy's eyes got as wide as saucers. He turned and ran.

She wanted to laugh. He must be a scaredy-cat instead of a tabby cat if a skinny thing like her could scare him.

Good-Looking Guy and Fiona had found a couple in matching monkey suits to pose for selfies with.

How appropriate.

She squatted down by Pim and pulled out the *Speak and Spell.* She asked again if he could tell the Skinwalkers from the Furies.

Pim pounced on the keyboard. "Bad Furries smell like blood," said the female synth voice.

"Okay, okay, good."

He put his nose in the air, sniffing.

"Not near now," he typed.

Fiona paused in her selfie-quest to stare at the *Speak and Spell*. "How is the machine talking? Is it a haunted toy?"

Nessa made an impatient sound. "Geez, put two and two together. It's my cat, Pim. He's invisible when he isn't in Werecat form."

"You do not really have an invisible cat!" Fiona declared.

"I kind of do," countered Nessa.

Fiona narrowed her eyes and looked down her nose. "Where did Barracuda find you? The 'Alice in Wonderland' ride at Disneyland?"

Nessa didn't answer. A spider web of shadows spun out from her feet to encircle all of them. Her whole body flared with heat.

She pulled in a breath and held it, her pulse pounding in her ears.

Good-Looking Guy noticed and quirked an eyebrow. "What?"

Grabbing Fiona with one hand and the *Speak and Spell* with the other, she pulled her in the direction of the emergency doors. They had to squeeze their way through massed groups of Furries. Pim hissed and lashed his tail, shadowing Nessa's steps.

People looked around as they felt him brush by. No time for explanations or clever lies.

"Something is going to happen," she said, choosing a spot and turning her back to the wall. "You should go and look for the Skinwalkers," she said to the guy. "I'm keeping Fiona with me."

"I think I'd rather go with him," said Fiona, trying to pull away. "He has a gun and you have a cray-cray look in your eyes."

"Gun," Nessa said derisively, "a lot of good that will do as already proven."

"What do you mean something is going to happen?" the guy said.

"The Skinwalkers laid down a threshold spell. That spell has compromised my shadow. I am going to have a visitor."

A shiver ran up and down her spine. Pim yowled. The ground beneath their feet shifted ever so slightly.

"Go or stay, dude!" she shouted. "Decide now."

He didn't move.

Nessa ripped off her backpack, unzipping it and grabbing the bag of salt inside. She flung the salt in a circle around them. The sharp-edged spell she spit to close it sliced her lips and she tasted blood.

Tabby was running their way, waving a hand.

Outside the circle, everything went dark.

Fiona started to protest.

Good-Looking Guy jerked her shoulder, "Quiet."

Good. He understood.

Her heart pounded and her eyes burned.

This had nothing to do with Fiona.

The monster was here for her.

CHAPTER FIVE

"Hello, darling," said the handsome man haloed in a shaft of white light as inky darkness blocked out everything beyond.

"Hello, Frank."

Pim hissed and spat, his back arched.

The man gestured at the circle of salt, "Really? Was this necessary? Aren't you happy to see me?"

Nessa said nothing. She pushed Good-Looking Guy and Fiona a little farther behind her.

"I couldn't help noticing you were here," said Frank, his voice rich as fine Belgian chocolate.

It was a deceptively simple sentence. She had spent much of her life trying not to be noticed by Frank. He had spent much of that same time pursuing the opposite.

He was tall, wide-shouldered, dark skin, black hair, strong features. Both manly handsome and girlishly beautiful at the same time. He wore a slim-fitting double-breasted wool suit, gunmetal gray, buttoned. His collared shirt was a dark blue and his tie a subtle blend of silver, gray, and blue. He looked like one of those too-gorgeous-to-be-real Bollywood action stars.

Except for the wings.

"I can see your mother in you. Such beauty and innocence," Frank said in his soft beguiling voice. "It's been months."

'Not long enough,' thought Nessa in despair.

He stroked his chin giving her a thoughtful once-over. "Your hair is a bit drab, though. What would you think about getting a few auburn or golden highlights? Tell me where you are. I can make an appointment at the best salon in the city. Hair, nails, reflexology. The lot. You deserve to be pampered...loved...honored for your gifts."

Again, she said nothing. Her throat was tight; she probably couldn't have spoken at that moment even if she wanted to.

Frank continued his appraisal, "And you're looking awfully thin. Is that ridiculous man who calls himself your father not feeding you?"

His name wasn't Frank, of course. Nessa suppressed his real name. Names gave power. He didn't need any more power over her.

The monster called Frank looked pointedly over Nessa's shoulder. "New boyfriend?"

Nessa did not rise to the bait. Good-Looking Guy wisely remained quiet.

The Bollywood-beautiful man wasn't really there. He was a projection. Frank had found her in a spiritual sense, not physical.

'Please God, don't let him know I'm in LA,' she pleaded silently, just in case God was listening because you never knew.

"Whoever he is, he doesn't deserve you." He had his hands in front of him and he used his long tapered fingers expressively. Beckoning to her. "I'm the one who loves you, Vanessa. And your mother misses you terribly. She longs for you, little one, with an aching sadness." His expression was one of pain and loss. "Let me bring her to you. We can be a family at last. What fun we can have."

The heat in her body had achieved meltdown status. Nessa felt her contacts dissolve as anger filled her.

"Fun," whispered Fiona. "We can have fun."

Crap.

She turned her head to hiss at Good-Looking Guy, "Cover her eyes. He can mesmerize her even in the circle."

A little gasp of surprise escaped his lips.

Nessa knew what he'd seen. The contacts were gone and her eyes were completely black. No iris, no pupil. Thanks to her mother's dark bargain with Frank, she'd been born that way. The cornflower blue contacts were to hide her eyes from the world. Hide the fact that part of her soul belonged to this creature.

Not all the descendants of heaven loved the light. Some chose darkness.

Frank's inky wings extended on a whoosh of icy air. They were not just black, each feather had the subtle shimmering gradations of a Peacock.

He began to sketch a series of sigils in the air.

Nessa recognized them.

She reached into her backpack and after a quick rummage, pulled out a plastic zip bag. Inside was a calligraphy brush with a long tapered head set in a pale carved handle. It wasn't ivory. The handle was made of bone. Human bone.

She held out her arm, pushing her sleeve to her elbow and held it out. Pim's strike was fast and deep, slicing open the skin. Blood welled in a thick line.

Behind Frank, a shimmering figure started to take form. A woman.

Nessa dipped the calligraphy brush in her blood. Whispering the spell, she began the runes for 'hidden' on the air itself. The blood did not drip. It didn't run. It hung suspended in scarlet streaks.

The woman's form grew more substantial. Small and slight as Nessa, long hair in perfect burnished blond waves framing a youthful, heart-shaped face and a little rosebud mouth. Her large blue eyes the same color as Nessa's contacts.

Genevieve Chevalier.

Dead nineteen years.

"Vanessa," her mother said.

Nessa's concentration faltered.

"Vanessa," she said again, holding her hands out. "My sweet girl, my baby."

Nessa forced her concentration back on the brush. Frank had done this to her before.

This time, however, another figure began to take shape. A little taller than her mom.

The woman had long gray hair piled perfectly on her head, a few tendrils artfully curled around her cheeks. She was old. Not that age mattered to Nessa, in her eyes the woman was beautiful. She was taller than either her daughter or granddaughter.

Her grandmother's face twisted in pain and fear. Her mouth moved but no sound came out.

Mom had known what she was doing — or thought she did — making a black bargain with a Fallen Angel. Her soul for power over the air at last. The magic had skipped a generation, as it sometimes does. Genevieve wanted what her mother had. Much good it did her. The maxim 'the House always wins' does not just apply to Las Vegas Casinos.

Frank had murdered Grandma Hattie two years ago. Took Nessa's grandmother's life out of spite after she learned his true name. Frank's true name gave Nessa a measure of power if... Well, if it ever came to that sort of fight.

Pim gave a heartrending meow, drawing the notes out. He'd loved Grandma Hattie as he now loved Nessa.

The scarlet streaks hovered in the air, pulsing with every beat of Nessa's heart, her hand frozen in mid-stroke.

Good-Looking Guy moved behind her. A strong, purposeful movement. She couldn't break her concentration to look. Couldn't risk her barrier tumbling down and Frank's hands around her soul.

Only when she saw the powder fly did she realize Good-Looking Guy was making his own magic circle. Spinning swiftly, something spilling from a small bag in his hands.

Not salt.

Nessa felt the chill of the grave.

The dead.

Corpse powder.

A dark-gray glow emanated from Good-Looking Guy's body as he forced his magic into the second circle. He activated it with a phrase that sent a shock of pain through Nessa.

It hit Pim at the same time and he hissed.

'Impressive,' Nessa thought in the small part of her brain not shaking in fear. Using magic within a magic circle was no simple feat.

Frank's face shifted, the benign look melting into a snarl, his eyes as black as her own.

"I grow tired of these games, child," he hissed. "You will be mine sooner rather than later."

Nessa felt the compulsion of her mother's voice and the phantom apparition of her Grandmother lift with the tingling burst of power from the corpse powder. With a final flourish, the blood rune was complete.

Nessa spoke its true name.

Light pressed against the darkness. Frank's well of shadows floated away and with a cry of rage, so did he.

Nessa fell to her knees, sucking in great gulps of air.

"Hey," said Good-Look Guy softly, kneeling by her. "Let me see."

He pulled out a navy-blue cotton handkerchief from his pants pocket.

Pim hissed and the guy waggled the handkerchief in the air vaguely in the direction of the invisible cat.

"Helping," he said.

Pim crouched lower, his tail snaking back and forth. Their Familiar bond meant he was feeling her pain and the lingering terror of Frank's appearance.

Nessa put one hand on his head. The cat gave her a searching look before stepping back.

"Was that your dad?" said Fiona with zero tact.

Nessa shook her head, not able to speak yet.

"He's killer gorgeous."

The blond certainly had the killer part right.

"And what was up with those wings?"

Fiona was behind her but Nessa imagined the witch fanning herself dramatically with one hand. She could have told Fiona that Frank was an Angel who had given himself to black magic. A Fallen. Could have said her mom sold her soul for power not knowing Nessa was growing in her womb, cursing her before she took her first breath. But she didn't. She kept quiet.

Her eyes had cooled but they were still black. They were always black. The contacts were to make her look normal. Custom-made and expensive.

With the makeshift bandage done, Nessa took several deep breaths and managed to get to her feet.

Good-Looking Guy handed her a pair of sunglasses from his tee-shirt pocket without a word.

She smiled her thanks.

"You need a proper bandage," he said. "I'm sure they have a first aid station. I think it's mandatory."

"No time," she said hoarsely and shoved the bone brush in the backpack. She'd have to cleanse it in saltwater later. No time now. "We've still got the Skinwalkers. Open your circle."

He wrote a sigil in the air she didn't know, whispered something that made the hair on the back of her neck stand on end and brushed an opening in the powder.

"Done."

She released the magic in her own circle.

Man-Child in his Tabby suit was standing at the edge of the salt. He didn't look frightened. He looked like a born-again Christian who had just seen Jesus walk on water.

"I saw the light," he said wide-eyed.

Nessa couldn't help adding sarcastically, "Praise the Lord!"

Good-Looking Guy laughed.

"The light and then shadow... poof." Tabby made a big movement with both hands. "You guys disappeared inside the shadow. Then there was rumbling and," he made the same motion, "it was gone. The shadow."

"Magic," whispered Good-Looking Guy with a Jazz Hands flourish.

"What..." Tabby started to say.

The guy shushed him, "Quiet, the grown-ups are talking." He put a hand on Nessa's shoulder. "Can I ask who that was?"

"No," she replied automatically and shrugged out of his grip. She wasn't big on strangers touching her.

"He saw me with you" he continued. "He thinks I'm your boyfriend."

"You're not my boyfriend."

"I could be," he laughed.

Nessa rolled her eyes. "Are you seriously flirting with me right now?"

He smiled. "No. Sorry. I mean he might think I could be and judging from what just went down, that's not a good thing. I feel like he's not a 'forgive and forget' sort of being."

"Frank," she said tersely.

"I'm sorry?"

"So am I," she said sincerely.

He chuckled. "I mean, I don't think I heard you correctly."

'No, it's Frank. At least that's what I call him. Can't say his real name. You know how that works.'

'Sure. Right.'

"I was born tied to him. Something happened in my mom's womb."

He spun her around. "Like in *Dune*? Paul Atreides creepy sister Alia?"

"What about *Dune*?" asked Tabby.

"Muad'Dib!" shouted Good-Looking Guy. He pumped a fist in the air,

Tabby did the same enthusiastically, "Muad'Dib!"

A couple of Furries nearby took up the chant automatically.

Nessa made a face. "Would you *not*, please! Oh my God. Geeks. I am not like Alia from *Dune* and the Bene Gesserat. I was not born omniscient. I was born with part of my infant soul tied in a knot in his deal with my mom."

"Muad'Dib!" shouted Tabby again.

Good-Looking Guy waved a cease and desist at him, "Past that now."

Tabby's face fell. "Oh."

"Okay, I get it," the guy nodded. "Demons are very big on contracts. As far as he was concerned, you came as part of the package."

Nessa didn't correct him. Better he thought she was tied to a demon than an angel.

"Do you have his number?" Fiona cut in.

Nessa stared at her. "His? Him?" She made a flapping motion with her arms. "With the wings? Are you totally clueless?

He would eat your soul for breakfast if you gave him half a chance."

"Yum," she said licking her lips.

Nessa threw her hands in the air. "That's it. I vote we give her to the Skinwalkers."

"Hey," Fiona pouted.

"Oh wait, I need to tell you," Tabby Cat said. "I finally found the guys to make the announcement. They wouldn't do it." He leaned closer, "I think money was involved, you know what I mean?"

No sooner had he said that than a large Furry reptile walking by stopped, did a double-take, and shouted, "Hey, it's her! Look!"

He pointed at Fiona.

Fiona took a photo of the fuzzy reptile.

"It is her!" A Wild Boar declared.

"I found her," said Reptile man.

"No, I found her first," said the Wild Boar bullying up belly-to-belly with the Reptile.

"Did not!"

"Did too!"

"Nobody found her," said a Black Bear stepping between them. "She was standing right here."

Pim yowled and Nessa followed his line of sight.

The Blue Wolf was already on them. He pounced from behind, grabbed Fiona around the arm and jerked her to him.

The Bear took exception to this.

"Back off!" said the Bear. "You weren't even near her." He pulled Fiona out of the Wolf's grip.

The Blue Wolf shoved the Bear.

Bear shoved him back, hard enough to throw him to the ground. It was a big bear.

Good-Looking Guy elbowed his way in just as shoving escalated into punches between the Bear, the Wild Boar, and the Wolf. In seconds the fighters were gleefully pounced on by another group of Furries who appeared to think this was part of the entertainment. There was a flurry of punches and kicks, few of which did much damage since the suits looked heavily padded.

The same could not be said of the Blue Wolf and Good-Looking Guy who had pulled apart and were pummeling each other.

A Leopard and something that looked like a Coyote moved in. They grabbed Fiona's arms and started to run. Or tried to.

Fiona dug in her feet and whacked the Coyote on the side of the head with her handbag. She turned and gave a hearty elbow to the Leopard's face.

She fought herself free for a moment before an assortment of furred and feathered Furries jumped on her with gleeful cries of "I win, I win!"

More and more Furries joined them, surging forward, paws reaching. Nessa was knocked off balance and fell to the floor. What had her dad used to say? 'Discretion is the better part of valor.' Sometimes he was right. She had better discretion her butt out of the way before it and the rest of her got crushed.

Crawling through a forest of furry legs and getting her fingers stepped on in the process, Nessa found a clear spot next to one of the vendor's tables. Holding onto the edge, she pulled herself up and froze.

Just on the other side of the table, two Furries went flying. Nessa smelled the hot, gunpowder scent of battle magic. Good-Looking Guy and the Blue Wolf were using magic.

Several other animals jumped bodily into the Good-Looking Guy's fight. That was not a good idea. What if the Witch Cop drew his gun and started shooting? Or the Skinwalker brought out his oh-so-sharp poison knife?

The Bear and the Wild Boar were back on their feet. They ran to the push and shove for possession of Fiona.

Directly in front of her, a separate pile of bright furry bodies seemed to be involved in another dispute entirely that had nothing to do with Fiona.

The ballroom had descended at the speed of light into furry chaos.

Nessa couldn't move, couldn't think, couldn't *breathe*. This was her fault. She'd done this. Mayhem followed her wherever she went. People could die and it would be her fault. Again.

CHAPTER SIX

Dropping like her strings had been cut, she put her forehead to her knees and wrapped her arms around her shins. The thud-thud-thudding of her heart was competing with the buzzing in her ears as her body tried to decide between passing out and a panic attack.

Panic attack seemed to be gaining the upper hand. It was hard to breathe.

A sandpaper lick to the skin of her arms and the muzzle of a soft, furry face pushed between her hands. She opened her eyes and for a moment the world moved in vertigo-inducing waves.

Oh crap.

She closed them again.

She did not want to throw up here in the ballroom. As if she wasn't making a big enough fool of herself already trying to be a grown-up bounty hunter. For fuck's sake, she could barely keep her clothes washed, her hair brushed, the toilet and sink clean, and make it to school in time for classes. Let alone play hide-and-seek with a black-winged Angel who wanted her soul.

Pim stood on his hind legs and head-butted her gently. He was feeling the panic zipping through her nervous system. He meowed softly and she felt him jump away. He was back in a few seconds.

She smelled cinnamon.

Nessa cracked open her eyes.

A churro.

Chocolate dipped at one end.

Stretching up, Pim set it on her knees. When she hesitated, he nudged it closer.

Taking a deep breath, she reached for the churro and took a bite.

Then another and another.

She chewed and swallowed and tried to ignore the yelling and tumbling bodies all around her.

The buzzing became more muted and though her heart still pounded, it didn't feel like it was going to burst out of her chest like an alien monster.

She broke off a piece of churro for Pim. An end with chocolate. Pim loved chocolate. He squatted on all fours to eat. Nessa absently ran her hand along his back. The fur stood on end and little sparks jumped from her fingers.

So many fuzzy Furries. So much static electricity.

Yes. So much.

The static electricity in the air was increasing exponentially from all the fighting, suffusing the ballroom from floor to ceiling. It even charged the polyester carpet. Norms couldn't feel it, all that rogue energy looking for an outlet. She could. And she knew from experience, positive and negative particles wanted to be released.

By the time the last bite of churro was chewed and swallowed, the sugar and carbs had worked their own form of magic. Nessa could take a deep breath and the world had stopped tilting to one side.

What she saw was not a good thing. Fiona was now hidden within a Furry throng. It must be Fiona because a cell phone was being held high in one slim well-manicured hand filming the whole show. The witch was probably already writing captions in her head for the Instagram story.

The group shuffled to the opposite side of the ballroom.

"Do you smell the tiger?" she asked Pim.

He nodded, pointing to Fiona.

Nessa reached under her shirt to the summoning belt strapped around her waist. Grandma Hattie had embroidered it when Nessa was seven. Runes for hot and cold air, positive and negative charges, thunder, lightning, storms, and several kinds of whirlwinds.

Each thread of every sigil on the belt had to be soaked in Nessa's blood for the summoning to be hers alone. There had been many tears that year. When Frank murdered Grandma Hattie, Nessa added her grandmother's silver air amulets corresponding to each rune. Air was the legacy of the Chevalier women from generation to generation. Except for her mom. What a cruel genetic anomaly that had turned out to be.

The belt not only boosted Nessa's spells, it protected her from any Elemental energy looking for a focus. As in, focusing through *her* body. The Elements were chaotic by nature and sometimes weirdly sentient. Nessa constantly walked a fine line between who and what was in control even with the belt.

"Wind it up!" she shouted to Good-Looking Guy who was still wrestling the Skinwalker. "We're getting out of here!"

Nessa ran her thumbs in a circle over the positive and negative amulets. Breathing in the energy sparking through the air, feeling it burn her lungs, silently speaking the names she would call on.

The Furries with Fiona came to a stop. They boosted her to the top of a table. She waved regally with one hand and took what looked like a panorama shot with the other.

A cheer went up and the group began shouting, "Fiona! Fiona!"

Nessa did a mental face plant.

"Tabby?" She glanced around for the Man Child in the cat-suit.

He was on the other side of the table looking worried.

"Are you okay?"

"I'll be fine but you'd better take off the kitty suit just for a minute."

His brows drew together. "Why?"

She let go of her Summoning Belt and imitated Good-Looking Guy's Jazz Hands move, "Magic!"

He grinned and started to undo some sort of zipper and hook fastenings on the side of the costume.

Nessa's chest had the familiar tight feeling as the magic grew inside her, making it hard to breathe. The names were anxious to be spoken. Energy always longed to be released. Chaos is Elemental Magic's natural form.

Good-Looking Guy hauled himself to her side. His deconstructed jacket was decidedly more deconstructed than the designer had intended. The white linen tee-shirt had ripped at the collar and was spotted with blood. One of his big brown eyes showed a swelling bruise.

He was breathing in noisy gulps and leaned heavily on the table.

"What's up?" he said hoarsely, running a shaky hand through his mussed hair.

"Wolf?"

"Down for now. Those guys are fucking immortal."

She outlined her plan and sent him on his way.

Pim arched his back hissing.

'Here we go,' Nessa thought.

Green Tiger, metal handcuff still dangling from his wrist, leaped in perfect apex predator form over the heads of the nearest

Furries landing next to Fiona. He reached for her and Nessa smacked her bracelets together releasing the spell with the spark.

Positive and negative electrons zeroed in on the Skinwalker and his metal handcuffs like lightning to a lightning rod.

The Tiger lit up like a Christmas tree. He screamed most impressively. The static electricity charge traveled through him and then jumped almost joyfully to every single person in a Furry suit and possibly nylon underwear.

There was a collective gasp as the electricity buzzed through hundreds of Furry nervous systems followed by screeches high, low, and everything in between. Her static charge wasn't enough to kill or even disable the norms. But it had to hurt like crazy and scare the hell out of them.

Good-Looking Guy yanked Fiona off the table and ran to Nessa.

The Green Tiger was vibrating and shaking, still caught in the grip of the main charge.

Nessa pulled herself together mentally and dashed for the emergency exits she'd seen at the back of the room. The doors were half-hidden behind a set of colorful banners for some video game. Tabby was next to her, dressed only in a pair of Avengers boxers and gazing wide-eyed at the mayhem.

She reached out a hand for the door then snatched it back swearing.

"This doesn't look good," Nessa said as Fiona and Good-Looking Guy caught up. She pointed at the door.

The guy groaned.

A circle of sigils was centered on each of the double doors leading outside.

Fiona, paying zero attention, reached for one of the door handles. A big sticker above it said: WARNING. Alarm Will Sound When Door Is Opened.

She managed to wrap her fingers around the handle before letting go and falling back with a cry.

"What's wrong?" asked the Tabby.

"The Skinwalkers, the ones after Fiona, her," she gestured at the blond witch who was blowing on her burned fingers, "have warded the doors with blood runes. We can't get through."

Pim hissed and arched his back, turning to the ballroom.

Nessa didn't need the *Speak and Spell* to know trouble was on the way.

Blue Wolf was staggering slowly in their direction.

Tabby said something that Nessa didn't hear due to the renewed pounding of blood in her ears.

"What?" she said.

"I could," said Tabby, "maybe."

"You could what?" asked Fiona. "Besides get out of here and leave us alone."

"I could get through the spell or whatever. I bet it only works on magic people. There's a Dungeons and Dragons scenario like that. Once the door is open, maybe you can go through."

Nessa stared at him in surprise. "That's absolutely a good idea, Tabby."

A smile stretched from ear–to–ear. "Tabby? Cool! I have a nickname! Does that mean I'm with the Scooby Gang?"

Fiona made a choking sound.

Nessa knew a good deal when she heard one. Putting a hand on his shoulder she said, "Totally! Scooby Dooby do it, Tabby!"

He stepped up to the doors, rubbed his hands together, and pressed the bar. The door swung open.

The fire alarm went off at the same time, just like the sign said it would.

He held the door and the three of them ran through. Tabby moved to follow.

"Get back inside," Nessa said pushing him, "run fast and put on your costume. Stay away from a Blue Wolf and Green Tiger. Okay?"

"Call me?" he said entreatingly as Nessa slammed the door shut.

The sigils would keep all magic users inside. Even those who set them up.

Of course, when some random norm pushed the doors open, the Skinwalkers could walk right through.

They'd come out at the back of the Center to a wide-open area marked in red for emergency vehicles. The main parking garage was about a hundred yards on their left.

"Where's your car?" she shouted to Fiona.

Fiona walked faster, saying nothing.

Nessa sighed noisily, 'She won't give you any trouble,' Barracuda said.

Yeah, right!

Pim transformed to Werecat form in one high jump. He ran ahead and smacked into a parking cone.

"You okay, buddy?" She motioned with one hand, "Go a bit more to your right."

Pim shook his head and adjusted his direction at a slightly slower pace.

Nessa reached inside her waistband to touch the Summoning Belt. With the thumb of her right hand, she traced first the rune and then the metal amulet for warm air.

Shifting to her other hand, she worked the cold air rune and amulet on the opposite side.

There was always warm and cold air circling somewhere in the atmosphere.

She kept the warm and cold fronts close, separate but ready. No need to mix them before the next threat made its grand entrance because she was one hundred percent sure they were not getting out without a fight.

"Hey! How do you kill a Skinwalker?" she asked jogging up to Good-Looking Guy.

"With death," he said not taking his eyes off Fiona.

Nessa did a quick rummage around her memory cells. He wasn't being sarcastic. "Corpse powder?"

"Yep. Put corpse powder in a human bone and encase it in lead. Shoot in a vital organ and you should have one dead Skinwalker."

"Don't suppose you have any of those handy."

He stopped as a car turned in front of them to enter the garage.

Fiona ran in front of the car nearly getting hit. She flipped a middle finger at the driver and barreled right past the garage entrance.

Where is she going?

"Sadly no. Much like dear Fiona, I was not expecting Skinwalkers in Torrance."

"But you have Corpse Powder," she said.

Fiona broke into a run.

Good-Looking Guy sped up. "Yeah. I have a lot of Grey Magic. You know, with the dead and ghosts? Corpse Powder is lighter than salt and I've found it more in tune with my spells. I've started always carrying a bag of it with me. I'm going to have to chase some nasty things."

"Don't you mean you *do* chase nasty things?" she corrected breathlessly.

He cleared his throat. "Uh, ha, ha, this is sort of my first case."

"No way," Nessa said before thinking, "mine too!"

"Really? I wouldn't have guessed."

"Will you two shut up!" screeched Fiona stopping to face them. "Nobody gives a fuck!"

The fire alarm kept them company as they ran along the side of the building. Nessa saw people up ahead. All of them were calmly walking out the front doors of the Center. Some Furries, some just regular people. The panicked rush Nessa was hoping for hadn't happened. No way to get lost in the crowd.

Sirens wailed in the distance.

Nessa jogged on until she caught up with the other two at a small parking area directly in front of the Center.

Handicapped parking.

Fiona beeped the locks on a shiny silver Audi sedan in a prime spot.

Nessa pointed accusingly at the plates. "You are so not handicapped!"

"Nor is she going anywhere," added Good-Looking Guy.

He was right. All four tires were slashed.

"Those bastards," yelled Fiona. "Do they know how much Michelin tires cost?"

"Pim!" Nessa shouted as he kept running ahead. "Get back here."

The Werecat stopped and peered myopically at the cars.

"Here, Kitty." Nessa waved both arms in the air for him, almost bringing the storm crashing together.

There was an ominous rumble overhead and the sky darkened.

Oops.

Good-Looking Guy spun on his heel. "Come on. My car." He took off in the direction of the garage.

Fiona followed, keeping pace with him easily with her long legs. Nessa waited for Pim then chased after them, struggling to keep up. Not only did she hate running, she was worn out from pulling magic out of thin air *and* she had to go to the bathroom.

Skipping the stairwell at the pedestrian entrance to the garage, Fiona and the guy barreled down the sloped entry ramp.

Turned out Nessa's lack of athletic skills was a good thing.

CHAPTER SEVEN

A large man stepped out from between two parked cars a couple of spaces inside the entrance and clocked Good-Looking Guy on the side of the head.

He went down in a heap.

The same guy grabbed Fiona. Nessa couldn't see what happened next but the big guy fell with a girlish scream and a few seconds later Fiona reappeared.

Her attacker did not get up.

She was handy with curses; Barracuda's file had said.

Fiona took off with what looked like a pair of keys in her hand. There was a '*beep beep*' from deeper in the garage.

Running became necessary. Nessa pursued, legs pumping, and slammed into something solid. Solid and furry.

She bounced off and fell backward onto her butt looking up into the snarling face of the Green Tiger. This was one tough bastard.

Tiger grabbed her shirt front and jerked Nessa to her feet. By that time, she'd already reached behind and unsnapped her expandable police baton from the clip on her jeans.

She used the momentum to slam the baton between his legs in a vicious arc. Skinwalkers, as far as she knew, were most often men. Balls were balls no matter what shape a guy took.

The Tiger's jaws dropped open and a gurgling moan dribbled out of his open mouth. Nessa wriggled out of his grip to bring the baton around to smack him in the knees. Hoping for one more hit, she backed up a step and raised her arm. Before she could strike, a blue paw grabbed her elbow and yanked.

Her arm turned at an excruciating angle and she fell, the pain shooting through her in nauseous waves. The world went dark for a moment.

Pim exploded onto the scene, jumping between Wolf and Tiger. The Tiger, wary of the werecat's poison claws and crouched at an awkward angle from Nessa's testicle strike, fell back. Pim turned his fury on the Wolf.

Blood spurted onto Nessa's face as her Familiar raked the Skinwalker with his scythe-like claws.

Pain and fear were good. No time to overthink. Just act. The agony in her arm pushed the spell even faster to her lips, pulling the nascent Elemental energy out of the air into her hands. She clapped the hot and cold air masses together. Electricity sparked zipping into the fluorescent lights and blowing them out one by one.

GIRL'S GUIDE TO VOODOO BOUNTY HUNTING 1

The Tiger tried to grab the Werecat by the scruff of the neck. Pim twisted around 180 degrees and bit.

The Tiger howled.

"To me!" she yelled at Pim.

Pim spun in an impossible somersault and landed at her feet. He spat out a furry green finger.

Nessa released the energy she had been holding and she and Pim dropped flat.

Hot and cold air in the right combination creates lightning. The energy smacked into the space between her two attackers and expanded. Physics plus magic is a wonderful thing.

They were lifted into the air and flung a dozen yards' end over end. One to the opposite side of the garage, the other to smack into the nearest wall with enough force to leave a wolf-sized imprint.

Belatedly, since sound is slower than light, the thunder hit with a sonorous boom setting off car alarms all over the garage.

A screech of tires was all the warning Nessa had as a black SUV hurtled down the exit lane between the parked cars. She rolled to the side. The car passed so close she could smell the burning rubber from the tires. Fiona was behind the wheel, Gucci sunglasses pulled down. The witch crashed through the payment gate sending splinters of the barrier flying.

On hands and knees, Nessa crawled to Good-Looking Guy. He was beginning to sit up, rubbing a lump on his head that was oozing blood.

"I don't feel so good," he moaned.

"If you throw up you'll feel better," said Nessa, speaking from experience.

He did and pulled himself to his feet pretty quickly after that.

"You're right, I feel better."

"Fiona stole your car," she said, brushing dirt off his expensive jacket.

He looked in the direction they'd been running. "That evil blond witch! This is your fault!" He waggled an accusing finger in her face. "If you hadn't grabbed her, the Skinwalkers would have taken her out and this would be over."

"I didn't know if there was a dead or alive clause in the Bail Bond contract," she admitted. "I'll ask Barracuda next time."

"If you don't catch her, maybe there won't be a next time."

Nessa's laugh had a bitter edge, "If only it were that simple."

Another car screamed up the exit ramp. A heavy black SUV.

The two of them fell over trying to get out of the way in time.

"I think those were the Skinwalkers," said Nessa rubbing her arm. Blue Wolf hadn't dislocated it but he'd come perilously close. Her elbow and shoulder hurt like crazy.

"No doubt."

Pim reverted to his kitty form and pulled at her leg. She slung the backpack around and gave him the *Speak and Spell*.

"Car," said the synth voice as Pim typed. "Track the car."

The guy stared at the *Speak and Spell*. "I think I can see him a little."

Nessa nodded knowingly. "You've probably got a concussion. Concussions and/or tequila seem to make him more visible to certain people. What color is he?"

"Uhhh, gray and white stripes?"

"Yep. Definitely a concussion."

Pim yowled, typing, "Are you listening?"

"Sorry," said the guy. "Car?"

"Do you have a tracking service?" synth voice intoned.

His eyes brightened. "Yes, yes I do. Through the coven."

"We'll take the scooter," said Nessa scooping up the *Speak and Spell* in one arm and Pim in the other.

CHAPTER EIGHT

With Good-Looking Guy squeezed behind her it was a tight fit on the scooter. She only had one helmet so they were just going to have to take their chances with the police. *Glamour* spells were not in her repertoire.

The Coven's version of On-Star picked up his car.

Nessa had her own tracking system. Barracuda's tether tugged at her. Urging her to find Fiona. He must have laid some sort of tracking spell on Nessa as well, damn it. All these tracking spells and the bail guy couldn't find her dad? What the hell?

"She's on Torrance Boulevard, heading North," he said, looking at the phone's screen.

"Probably making for the 110," Nessa shouted over the whine of the engine.

Fiona said her house was in Glendale. That was the most direct way through downtown from here.

Damn.

It would take ages for Nessa to get across the city by surface streets. No way could she follow the witch on the freeway. The scooter barely pushed forty-five at the best of times. CHP would spot her for sure. Or more likely she'd get hit by a truck and die an ingloriously mundane death.

They zipped ahead on Torrance Boulevard, Nessa leaning low over the handlebars as if that would help the scooter go faster.

"Keep going," he yelled by her ear as they burned through yellow lights and careened around parked cars. "She didn't get on the freeway. Take a right on Figueroa."

Figueroa? What the heck? Where was she going?

They passed several pile-ups full of crumpled fenders and steaming tempers.

"I bet that's from our girl!" said the guy.

Pim meowed in agreement.

It became apparent Fiona was not going anywhere near Glendale. She was heading west for the low-rent, high-crime neighborhoods. That direction included... Nessa laid out a map of LA in her mind. That included Compton. Compton?

The runaway witch stayed on surface streets and, according to the GPS, Nessa and Good-Looking Guy were gaining.

"We're almost on top of her," he shouted.

How was that possible? Unless Fiona had stopped. Which, they soon discovered, she had. Though not by choice.

Under a section of the 91 Freeway, they found a stand-off. The black SUV had been forced through a section of hurricane fencing into what looked like a storage area for road work equipment. The SUV was blocking the way out, wedged between a backhoe and a cherry picker.

Skinwalkers versus Fiona. Two against one.

It had been three against one. One member of the gang was face down in a pool of blood.

Point for Team Fiona.

Perhaps Skinwalkers in their human form were a bit more vulnerable or maybe this was just another human henchman. The guy she'd cursed at the parking lot certainly hadn't stood up again.

Fiona's gun was aimed steadily at the two Skinwalkers still in front of her. They seemed to be deciding who was going to rush her first.

And where did she even get a gun? It looked too big to fit in the Gucci bag.

Nessa slowed and Good-Looking Guy did a cool movie-cop style jump from the back of the scooter. He had his gun in one hand.

Nessa didn't know anything about guns except the point-shoot-you're-dead part. Her dad was a Con Artist who chose to live by his magical wits — the few he had.

Nessa thought she might be forgiven by Barracuda for revving the scooter's engine and doing a gravel spewing about-face with the idea of getting the hell away as far and fast as she could. Worksite shoot-outs were not in her skill set. At least not yet.

Pim stuck one paw through the basket and pointed frantically at the road, meowing a kitty version of, 'Let's get out of here!'

She made it halfway down the block before Barracuda's tether jerked. She gagged and clenched the brakes with both hands. Pim made a choking sound from the basket.

Just how smart was this dang tracking spell? She tried scooting a few more yards. The invisible noose tightened again.

Too smart.

Barracuda's voodoo magic was determined to do what her conscience would not: Finish the job and bring the annoying Fiona in.

Damn and double damn.

She turned the scooter around.

Cautiously approaching the storage site, she quickly realized no one was paying any attention to her at all. The whole group was engaged in a shoot-out worthy of cable TV. Guns banged and popped depending on the caliber and bullets pinged off metal or thunked into the concrete overpass.

Magic was all very well but guns could kill you faster and more efficiently. Nessa was sure enough bullets would take even the Skinwalkers time to recover from. Of course, in the interim, you could always cut off their head. That should stop them.

She shuddered and backed away fast from that mental picture.

The heavy SUV still blocked the way between the backhoe and the cherry picker. Too bad she didn't have Pansy and Rose Marie as backup. They could probably lift the oversized vehicle out of the way.

Then she realized its position could work to her advantage.

Taking a page from the Skinwalker's playbook, she told Pim what to do. His body rippled and space seemed to bend around the stocky cat as he transformed to his larger, meaner alter ego.

Seconds later a soft hiss of air was followed with four heavy *thunks*. Those premium Bridgestone tires were now history.

Nessa stepped off the scooter and marked off an area near the broken hurricane fencing with salt leaving a small bit open. She barely had enough. It had been a rather salt-intensive day. With the sigil on her belt, she summoned a whirlwind, anchoring it inside with three hastily drawn chalk sigils and several drops of her blood. Finger-pricking thingies for diabetics were a godsend for witches.

Pim crept back to her. Nessa gunned the scooter as he jumped into the basket. She wove between the oversized machines staying near the fence line and hopefully out of sight. She came up behind the Witch Cop's hijacked SUV. The back was open and from what Nessa could see the guy had an arsenal in there. Now she understood where Fiona got the gun. Fiona and the guy were keeping the Skinwalkers to the cover of a yellow backhoe with help from rapid-fire automatic weapons

They couldn't stay there forever.

"Don't shoot me!" she yelled, announcing her presence. They looked around wildly for a second before spotting her.

"Come on, Fiona. Get on!" She pointed at Good-Looking Guy, "And you too!"

They both hesitated.

"You are boxed in. This will not end well. Come on!"

Good-Looking Guy tossed the machine-gun-style weapon he was holding and hopped on the back. He motioned for Fiona who looked at them doubtfully.

"He can hold you," Nessa said.

The witch threw herself into the guy's arms, her long legs dangling over the side of the bike.

Nessa revved the scooter and took the same path around the outside between the hurricane fence and the machinery. The scooter wobbled and she swore, shifting her weight to keep it upright. Bullets pinged off the machinery as the Skinwalkers tried to pick them off.

Nessa was just in front of the torn fencing and the way out when the Blue Wolf gave a mighty leap up and over the Escalade to block the entrance. Exactly where she hoped he would.

He landed in her circle. Sweeping one foot through the salt, she closed the circle and spoke the words. The magic went rogue without her to anchor it inside. The wind she'd trapped in the circle picked up the wolf and spun him in dizzying loops. He'd be stuck there until someone broke the circle.

They squeezed by, just barely making it through the narrow opening. Nessa revved the scooter and took off up the road.

CHAPTER NINE

Good-Looking Guy held Fiona in his arms and Fiona had a stranglehold around Nessa's neck as the Scooter wove a wobbly pace through the unfamiliar streets. They looked like a circus act. The scooter was doing maybe thirty, the engine whining loudly in protest.

"Where were you going?" asked Nessa. "And where are we going to go now?"

"I figured I would head for Barracuda's," said Fiona, straining her voice to **be** heard. "He would want to protect his investment."

"Good move," said the guy just as loudly. "Paperwork for dead bail jumpers is a bitch."

'How do we get there from here?' was the next obvious question. Unfortunately, before she could ask it, a horrible metallic screaming made her cringe, sending shivers down her spine. The Escalade was on their mechanically-compromised tail.

They were running on rims, the metal spewing sparks as it accelerated in pursuit.

She whipped over to the other side of the street and with a butt-busting jump, up onto the sidewalk. Somebody threw a soft drink can at her as she steered perilously along the sidewalk. All the people cleared off behind closed doors seconds after seeing the **Escalade**. This was a neighborhood that understood danger.

The Escalade shadowed them from the street. The windows slid down and she saw Green Tiger in the front seat. Maybe Blue Wolf was still airborne.

Sun glinted off the barrel of a gun.

Fiona saw it too and gave a strangled, "*Eeep*."

Nessa couldn't call up a spell, she had her hands full trying to keep them from crashing. Besides she was pretty much magic'd out after the series of stormy summonings.

And if she did not find a bathroom soon there was going to be serious trouble.

Pim pawed at the basket, trying to undo the latch. He had changed back to kitty form to reduce weight on the bike.

Good-Looking Guy had his pistol out, the barrel waving around as Fiona squirmed and Nessa attempted to steer.

A group of big guys on mucho-macho motorcycles roared up to the Escalade surprising the hell out of Nessa who nearly lost control of her bladder. The scooter pitched dangerously from side to side before she somehow got it balanced.

The bikers had guns, too, but didn't open fire. This was a residential street. Houses lining both sides. Maneuvering expertly, they formed an escort on both sides of the big SUV, weapons aimed at the windows.

The Escalade driver slammed the brakes. The big bikes sped by on their forward momentum.

Nessa heard more than saw the screech of metal as the Escalade did a one-eighty — not easy to accomplish on rims — to head back the way it had come. A couple of the motorcyclists peeled out in pursuit. The others stayed behind, slowing. One rider beckoned for Nessa to come to the street.

She was in no position to argue.

Bumping down the nearest driveway, she cruised over. The bikes slowed to keep pace in front and behind.

Pim finally succeeded in undoing the latch on the basket and popped up. He gave her a big-eyed stare and she told him, "Wait."

If the bikers attacked, he could shift.

They came to a stop in the middle of the street.

"What the hell are you bringing to our neighborhood?" demanded the man on the lead bike. He was big, like bodybuilder big. Dark, strong jaw, hooked nose. She couldn't see his eyes behind the mirrored aviators. His leather jacket has a patch on the front: Crusaders. The picture was of a skeleton in armor.

Not too hard to guess they were currently in Crusader territory.

Neither Good-Looking Guy nor Fiona answered so Nessa spoke up.

"They were chasing us. I'm sorry. We didn't mean to cause you any trouble."

"Was one of them in a fuzzy costume?" The lead biker asked. "Or am I seein' things?"

Nessa had planted both feet on the ground and was desperately trying to keep the scooter from falling over. It kept swaying from side to side with the unbalanced load. "What? Fuzzy? Yep. Yes. Two, actually. Kind of crazy. They ran her," Nessa tipped her head back to indicate Fiona, "off the road and wrecked her car."

"And that brought you three white people to my block because?"

"Hey, I protest being called white!" Good-Looking Guy said.

"White is not only a shade but a state of mind," said an equally large man on the bike just behind the leader.

"Truth," said the man in front. He twisted around for a hand bump.

Pim gave a hair-raising howl of frustration and as if on cue, all the bikers' eyes turned to the basket.

"What in the name of holy Jesus was that?" asked the biker.

Sometimes you just have to tell the truth.

"I have an invisible cat."

"She does," said Fiona, nodding enthusiastically and almost unbalancing Nessa's precarious hold on the scooter.

"White can also be a state of mental instability," said the philosopher on the second bike.

Pim yowled again. Nessa knew that tone of voice. These guys were a threat and he did not like people threatening his mistress. He was going to transform if they didn't get out of this situation soon.

"We're heading for Barracuda Bail Bonds," she said in a rush. "I work for him."

"You do not!" laughed the lead biker. Several of the others joined in. "You about the size of a postage stamp, what you gonna' do for the likes of that man?"

"My invisible cat," Pim meowed heartily, "and I do so work for Mr. Barracuda. We started today. We're the new bounty hunters. Like Pansy and Rose Marie. Only smaller. We're replacing some guy that got whacked with a machete."

The big biker put his hand over his heart, "May Victor Alonzo rest in peace."

"Amen," said the biker behind.

"Anyway, um, that's where we're going. Barracuda Bail Bonds."

He pursed his lips, "Barracuda is my cousin." He looked at her suspiciously. "If you know Barracuda, then tell me. Who does he serve?"

"Legba," answered Nessa, hoping that's the answer he was looking for.

He nodded. "Correct. And who do you serve, little postage stamp?"

Whoa. Now there was a question. Who did she serve? Her belief in God waxed and waned depending on how terrified she was. Her father was nothing but self-serving. Her Aunt Emerald could probably be said to serve the gods of avarice. There had only been one other steady influence in her life.

"I follow what my Grandmother taught me about the spirits of the air. Or at least I try to. Most of the time," she added lamely. Today's shenanigans would not have met with her Grandmother's approval. Not at all. She said as much to the biker.

He cocked his head to one side and gave her an appreciative stare. "Well okay then, postage stamp. I approve of someone who respects their Grandmother. Guess we will be seeing you all around the neighborhood."

"Not me!" piped up Fiona, squirming in Good-Looking Guy's arms. "I live in Glendale."

"Shut up," hissed Good-Looking Guy.

"Can you tell me how to get to Barracuda's from here? I got a little turned around and we sort of got our hands full."

"You don't want to ask your invisible cat?" said the lead biker.

Several guys behind him sniggered.

Nessa brightened. Precariously shifting the backpack, she removed the *Speak and Spell* and set it in the basket.

"Pim, do you know where the Bail Bonds office is from here?"

Pim chirped a series of conversational meows as he typed.

"I'm not sure," said the toneless synth voice.

The bikers watched with open mouths.

"We're close. I smell hamburgers. Nessa, I want a hamburger. Now."

The lead biker burst into a laugh that went on so long he started to cough and wheeze.

"That's a hungry invisible cat! There's a Carl's Junior two blocks from here. Follow that freckled nose and your invisible cat along the 91. Y'all will see a Carl's Junior. Get that cat a hamburger. After Carl's, take a right, you'll find Barracuda's soon enough."

He revved his engine so loudly it made Nessa's eyes water.

She put the *Speak and Spell* away and said thank you except he probably couldn't hear her over the noise of the engines. The lead guy sketched her a salute and the gang sped off with a deafening roar and a blast of heat exhaust.

Nessa revved her engine far less dramatically and the scooter wheezed up the street.

They stopped at the Carl's Jr. because Nessa declared she had to go to the bathroom "Or else!" Plus, it was her scooter and she and Pim wanted hamburgers.

When she came out of the lady's room feeling much, much, better, Good-Looking Guy stood near the counter holding a receipt and Fiona was sipping a large drink.

"Where's mine?" she asked the guy.

He at least had the manners to look embarrassed.

"You didn't order me anything?"

"I didn't know what's you wanted," he said shrugging.

"That is the lamest excuse there is. People always say that when they can't be bothered to be nice."

Nessa ordered a double burger with cheese for her and one for Pim without lettuce and tomato. Her cat was not a fan of vegetables.

She sat at one of the tables and ate as fast as she could which was admittedly not very fast. Her gag reflex kicked in when she was stressed and she was plenty stressed right now. Eating slowly kept her from throwing up. Generally.

The other diners looked at them with slightly confused, 'How did you get here?' looks. Not antagonistic. Just curious.

Poor Pim was forced to eat his burger in hiding under the table. A situation not to his liking. Pim was a proper seat-at-the-table sort of feline. Nessa apologized, explaining floating hamburgers were not the sort of attention they needed at this moment.

Between bites, Nessa kept a lookout for the black Escalade. Fiona looked at nothing but her phone. Good-Looking Guy stood outside talking on his cell and hopefully keeping an eye on her scooter.

Pim hopped up beside her. He growled quietly, low in his chest. He expected more trouble. So did she.

Fifteen minutes' start-to-finish and they piled back circus-clown style on the scooter, much to the amusement of the fast-food patrons and staff. A few people even clapped as they wobbled in the direction of Barracuda Bail Bonds.

They rounded a corner and there it was. Barracuda's bright green teeth-snapping neon sign. The driveway to the little yellow bungalow was within spitting distance when the SUV ground up the street, somehow still mobile on its rims.

Maybe Skinwalkers had SUV levitation magic. They were certainly good trackers, Nessa had to give them that.

The heavy car caught them easily, swerving in to clip the back of the scooter, sending it into a wild spin. They spilled onto the street in a tumble of arms, legs, and obscenities.

Nessa felt fuzzy and unfocussed from the fall. She sat in the street and rubbed the back of her head. Both knees throbbed. Her jeans were ripped and her shoulder ached.

Fiona was close. She could see that. The witch had one hand wrapped around a bleeding shin and with the other was writing a glowing sigil in the air. The power of the mark radiated to where Nessa lay half-sprawled across the running board. Battle magic.

Pim howled in protest and she scooted painfully around to look at him. The bike had landed at an odd angle making it difficult for Pim to reach the fastener on top of his basket. His claws pawed at it frantically, trying to catch the hook.

She needed to crawl over and help him but her body felt so heavy like gravity was acting up again.

Good-Looking Guy had his back to her. He was just pulling himself up to his hands and knees when the Escalade jumped the curb and screamed to a stop.

Green Tiger and Blue Wolf, the wolf looking extremely rough, piled out, their fur bristling with anger.

Her eyes automatically went to Green Tiger's hand/paws. He was missing the ring finger on the left one. The same hand from which dangled her handcuffs.

His expression made it clear Nessa was going to pay for that.

The front door of the Bail Bonds office swung open. Barracuda, Pansy, and Rose Marie stepped out on the porch.

Help had arrived.

They stopped.

Maybe?

The three of them stood in a line in identical poses, arms crossed over their chests.

Or not.

They didn't look like they were going to interfere. Was it a test to see if she could fight? She'd used her magic in a lot of odd situations. For years, her dad had toured the country with Nessa in tow as a rainmaker. Scamming farmers was one thing, hand-to-hand combat, quite another. A five-foot-two girl and a police baton could only go so far in a fight.

There was no time to wait for them to make up their minds. The Tiger turned on her and the Wolf charged Fiona and Good-Looking Guy.

Nessa panicked and ran, heading for the Escalade. The door was open and she leaped through the driver's side closed the door and slammed her hand on the locks.

The Tiger stood staring through the windshield, his lips curled back in a snarl. A scary snarl that showed big teeth. He pulled one fist back and smashed it through the tempered glass.

Nessa screeched in surprise and was very glad she had gone to the bathroom back at Carl's Junior.

Through the broken glass, Nessa heard more than saw Pim had succeeded in opening the latch on the basket. There was a howl that made even her hair stand on end.

The Tiger punched another hole and more glass shattered around his fist. Nessa tumbled from the front seat to the back. He reached through and grabbed her foot before she could get away. With a squeal, she struggled and managed to kick off her faded Chuck Taylor. Thank God it wasn't a high top or he'd have had her for sure.

The Tiger roared and tossed the shoe at her, knocking her on the side of the head. Grabbing the glass, he peeled away the entire windshield as easy as pulling off a band-aid. In a second, he was up on the hood and climbing through.

Nessa unlocked the back door and fell more than stepped out onto the street, bruising her tailbone. She yelped. It felt like she'd broken her butt.

Frantically getting to her feet — one shoe on, one shoe off — she limp-ran to the back bumper and clambered up. Her skinned knees burned at the fresh assault and her stupid sock went sliding on the slick metal. Adrenalin and panic somehow got her up and onto the roof.

A frantic glance around showed Fiona had the Wolf locked in some sort of wrestling move that involved tangling her arms and legs with his into a sailor-worthy knot.

Fiona? Wrestling? Nessa never would have seen that coming!

Good-Looking Guy was straddling the Wolf, his knees around the beast's throat. One hand gripped the Skinwalker's pointy ears to tip his head back and he was emptying something down its throat with the other.

That was all Nessa had time to take in before the Tiger joined her, leaping from the sidewalk to the top of the Escalade in an effortless jump. The vehicle rocked under his weight.

Nessa had been chased by Frank all her life. You'd think she'd be used to it. Well, she was learning today that someone pursuing you with spirit magic was very different from scary monsters with big teeth menacing you from a few feet away.

For a heart thudding moment, Nessa stood, completely out of ideas. The fear slowing her brain to a crawl.

Pim jumped between them in full werecat form. Back arched and yowling.

The Skinwalker paused to reach into a beaded gondolier style leather pouch around his chest. A medicine bag. A tradition among many Native American people. Nessa knew that much. This could only be bad medicine.

A flick of the wrist and a burst of powder sped through the air. The powder enveloped Pim in a dense yellow cloud. He began to sneeze uncontrollably.

'Air?' Nessa thought, her head clearing.

Air she could handle.

She touched the silver whirlwind amulet. Her other hand drew the sigil to summon the wind. The tempest flowed through her, tossing her hair in a burst of cold air. It rushed past Pim, taking the medicine pouch powder with it and throwing it back to encircle the Skinwalker. He cursed and flailed his arms, convulsed momentarily in a choking cough.

Gathering the air around her she heaved a second blast, hoping the wind's momentum would push him off the roof.

Still coughing, he had the wits to dig in with the claws on his feet. They pierced the metal, caught, and held. He dissipated the dust with a hoarse chant.

Nessa leaned over, her hands on her knees trying to catch her breath. Hamburger or not, her magical energy meter was running on fumes. Her head spinning; her knees shaking.

This job was either going to make her into one kick-ass adult Witch or it was going to kill her.

The Tiger leaped easily over Pim, arms outstretched.

Probably kill her...

He wrapped one big paw around Nessa's jacket and the next second she was flying head over heels through the air.

She landed hard on the dry brown grass of Barracuda's front lawn.

Pim jumped after her. Stiff-legged, he stalked between her and the Green Tiger. A high-pitched yowl came from his throat, daring the Tiger to attack. Nessa unclipped her police baton, her hands trembling. She could feel warm blood running over her mouth and chin.

"Hold on, little brother," said a deep, resonant voice.

Rubbing her eyes and trying to get the double images to merge into one, she saw Barracuda had stepped off the porch to stand on the lawn. Somehow he was now between her and the Green Tiger. She hadn't even seen him move.

He was also holding a spear.

CHAPTER TEN

The granny glasses were gone and his eyes glowed emerald green, every bit as bright as the neon sign in the front yard. Barracuda was channeling his Voodoo royal blood.

Barracuda held his hand out, "Wait but a moment."

It took Nessa a few heartbeats to realize he was speaking to Pim, not the Tiger. The werecat's tail lashed furiously back and forth and his muscles were tensed to spring but he paused.

Barracuda faced the Skinwalker. "You dare cross my boundary?"

He struck the ground with the butt of his spear, and it boomed like a kettle drum.

"Threaten my staff?"

He smacked the spear into the ground again.

"Hit this little girl?"

This time the boom sounded like the crash of thunder.

"I'm not a little girl," Nessa said irritably, wiping the blood off her face with the back of her hand.

Barracuda turned his headlight bright gaze on her.

"Let the man do his business, child," admonished one of the women on the porch.

Nessa put a hand over her mouth and Barracuda turned back to face the Tiger.

He was standing up for her. This was a good thing.

"I'm a child," she said in a little voice, "such a child. And he hurt me," she added with a dramatic sob that would have made her scam-artist father proud

Barracuda's eyes glowed even brighter.

"A child!" he thundered. "A girl child! And you a grown man hiding in that animal's skin!"

"Yeah, a girl child," she echoed, sniffling and shoving the police baton behind her back.

The Skinwalker had summoned a cloud of black spells. He raised them high in his hands. "Don't get in my way fat man. This child owes me blood."

"Fat?" said Barracuda.

"Uh oh," Nessa heard in chorus from Pansy and Rose Marie on the porch. "He used the 'F' word."

The Tiger curled his lip. "Yeah. Fat. Fat man had better move his fat ass or I will take him down with her."

He pulled his hands back and pitched the ball of spells directly at Nessa. Nessa put her wrists up hoping to deflect the worst of the magical blow and shut her eyes.

After one breath and then another, when nothing had smashed her into bloody bits, she opened them.

The ball of spells hovered a few feet away, buzzing angrily. Barracuda's spear was pointed straight at the boiling, inky mass, holding it immobile.

With what looked like the barest effort, the Voodoo King swung the spear at the Tiger forcing the spells to follow. The black ball crashed into its summoner, bursting into flames on his chest.

The Tiger roared, crouching in feral grace and menace, his yellow eyes on Barracuda.

The beating of drums filled the yard.

The Tiger leaped for Barracuda. His mouth wide, claws ready to rip and tear.

Barracuda didn't move. Didn't flinch.

He struck the butt of the spear on the ground a third time.

Bony arms burst up from the yard, a dozen or more. They grabbed the Tiger's legs and jerked him back to earth.

Barracuda's eyes glowed with menace and when he spoke, his words blazed with light.

Nessa didn't recognize the language. She didn't need to. Their terrifying intent was clear. Cowering to the ground she covered her ears. Pim ran and crawled under her chest and she shifted her hands to cover his head. Whatever she heard, for him it was a dozen times worse.

The Skinwalker fought, struggling desperately to break free. He clawed at the ground. He roared. He swore. It looked at one point like he was trying to change back into a human but he could not escape the death grip of the bones.

He sank into the ground, his cry of terror cut off by the churning earth.

Feeling light-headed Nessa sat up staring at the front yard. Her mouth tasted like blood and her throat was too dry to swallow. Pim gave a tremulous meow. Under the force of the spell, he had changed back to his invisible self.

Barracuda stood very still. His eyes slowly dimmed and the bright aura around him faded.

Nessa watched as the turf unnervingly smoothed itself over.

"Shouldn't have called him fat," said one of the ladies on the porch.

"Guess not," said Nessa in a whisper.

A small section of brown grass suddenly split open. Nessa and Pim both scooted back. The ground rumbled and a pair of metal handcuffs shot up like they were fired by an air gun. They caught a beam of the late afternoon sun and shone with a silver light.

Nessa put her hand out and the cuffs fell neatly into her palm. The earth closed and smoothed itself over once more.

Good-Looking Guy and Fiona limped over from the other side of the SUV. Both Fiona's shins were bloody and she had what looked like the beginning of a black eye.

The guy was bloodied and bruised and his deconstructed jacket had finally self-destructed.

He had her Chuck Taylor and waved it in the air.

"Thanks," she said, taking the shoe. "What did you put in the Skinwalker's mouth?"

"Corpse powder. I hoped it would choke him." He glanced over his shoulder. Nessa could just see the wolf's feet. It lay still. "At least it's keeping him quiet. I'm Ravi, by the way. Ravi Singh. After surviving the day's mayhem, I feel we should introduce ourselves."

"Ravi," she repeated.

"It's like the Indian version of Michael," he said with an easy laugh. "Everyone knows a Ravi."

"I'm Nessa Scott and my cat is Pim." She held up the handcuffs and waggled them. "Well, Ravi Singh, notice anything?"

He looked at her blankly.

"When we handcuffed Mr. Tiger back at the Event Center, I put one cuff on his left wrist. Your job was to fasten his right wrist around the railing." She waggled the cuffs again. "Your ring wasn't locked all the way. That's how he just waltzed into the ballroom looking for us with the cuffs dangling from his left, I repeat *left* wrist."

He started to protest, seemed to think better of it, and gave her a sheepish smile. "Oops."

"Oops?" Nessa glared at him. "You are a Witch Cop. Kind of think you're supposed to have a handle on the whole handcuff thing."

"*Ooooo* she got you there, pretty boy!" jeered Pansy. Nessa thought it was Pansy. She seemed to stand on the left and Rose Marie on the right.

His smile stayed in place but his tone became somewhat accusing, "Well, Miss Voodoo Bounty Hunter, if you'd let the Furry poison her with his cursed knife back in the Sequoia Room, all this could have been avoided."

"Hey," protested Fiona punching him in the arm. "Not cool!"

The Sequoia Room! Her heart did a double-thump. "Oh my God. We left the DMA guys in the basement back in Torrance."

Fiona snorted a laugh. "Maybe the Skinwalker ate them."

"No. No eating and no bodies," Ravi said calmly. "Todd, you know the guy with the goatee?" He made a motion on his chin like drawing a beard.

Nessa nodded, she remembered.

"After I shot the Skinwalker, he threw a hella' strong circle around the whole group. Pretty sure they are fine."

"Awesome," she said sincerely. Nessa did not want any more souls on her conscience.

"Damn," said Fiona with equal sincerity. "Too bad."

Nessa retrieved her scooter, setting it on the kickstand in the driveway. The scooter had survived the crash with little damage except the mirror popping off. It did that a lot and she had it screwed back on under Pim's supervision in no time.

Barracuda joined her. He pointed the spear at Nessa.

"What's wrong with your eyes?"

Nessa automatically jumped to one side. That thing radiated a dark power she had no desire to be in front of.

"They always look like this. I burned through my contacts back at in Torrance. Witch Cop gave me a pair of sunglasses to use."

She felt on her head and looked around. Where had they gone?

She spied them on the grass and ran to pick them up.

Barracuda made a *'tch, tch'* sound, saying, "See you replace them. You gonna' scare the customers like that."

"I'm going to scare the customers?" Nessa said sarcastically, gesturing at the yard, Barracuda, and the very large, non-human twins. "*Me?*"

He snorted.

Pansy, maybe, she and her twin were not in line so Nessa wasn't sure, joined them. She handed Fiona a black motorcycle helmet covered in *STP* and *Pennzoil* stickers.

Her new boss pointed imperiously to the street. "Get your skinny scooter on the road," he barked, "and take this young woman and deliver her to the Tribunal."

Nessa looked at him blankly.

"Go on! You got a job to do, girl."

Right, deliver Fiona. Get the slip, whatever that was, from whoever was supposed to hand it over and bring it back here.

Fiona, much to Nessa's surprise did not object. She seemed to believe, as the Shaman had done, the tribunal would let her off with a wrist slap despite missing the Monday meeting.

"They'll add three more months of those stupid DMA meetings," she said bitterly, strapping on the helmet. "Mummy is a Council member as were all the Gardes, three generations and counting." She gave Nessa a smug smile.

'Three generations and counting,' mimed Nessa in her head. Stuck up.

"I want that helmet back," he said to Nessa as he handed her a ten-dollar bill. "And get yourself some gas. Don't you go losin' the slip from the Tribunal because you had to walk back from Redondo Beach."

As she turned on the scooter's engine, a black SUV identical to the one Fiona stole from Mr. Ravi 'Witch Cop' Singh pulled up in front of the driveway. A tall woman with long dark hair pulled back in a ponytail and wearing dark glasses got out.

Nessa paused, wanting to see what happened next.

The woman, dressed in a mannish suit so that she looked a lot like Will Smith in *Men in Black,* pulled out an armful of iron manacles.

She and Ravi proceeded to chain every movable part of the Skinwalker and toss him in a heavy cage in the back-bed of the car.

Pansy and Rose Marie stood with their boss on the sidewalk watching.

"That is one fine-looking enforcer," said one of the twins. "He can enforce any rule he wants with me."

"Stand in line!" said her sister.

They high-fived each other.

Barracuda watched the loading process, nodding in approval.

"Now these are people who understand how to transport miscreants." He looked pointedly at Nessa.

"Hey," she said staring up at him and patting the scooter's handlebars, "it got us here, didn't it?"

He sniffed. Clearly not impressed.

"Let's go," Fiona said, tapping the top of Nessa's helmet. "Tribunals to annoy, auto club to call, shit to do in a better part of town and with better-dressed people."

Pim meowed from the front basket in what sounded like agreement.

Nessa revved the engine and they sputtered up the street.

Redondo Beach is not far from Compton on a LA map but with every muscle aching, it felt like it took forever to Nessa. After dropping off Fiona and picking up the all-important slip, Pim curled into a tight furry ball in the basket and fell asleep. Nessa wished she could do the same.

With the sun, had gone the warmth. In California, the temperature inevitably dropped as darkness settled on the coast. Nessa's escape bag was at the Bail Bonds office and with it, her light parka. Zipping along the Pacific Coast Highway in a polyester Uniqlo hoodie was a chilly business.

Her teeth were chattering by the time she locked the bike to the blinking barracuda and its glowing dollar-sign eyes.

Light poured out the barred windows of the yellow bungalow and there was a burst of laughter from inside.

Nessa and Pim walked slowly up the three steps to the porch. She opened the front door and the wonderful smell of hot pizza wafted out.

"Get yourself in here girl," said Barracuda still laughing over something Pansy or Rose Marie had said. He was standing at a square table with four dining chairs on the other side of the office. Nessa hadn't noticed it before. Two large pizza boxes covered most of the table's surface.

The stereo was playing an Earth Wind and Fire song. Nessa had a classical music education courtesy of her father. Classic rock, that is.

"Close that door cuz you're lettin' in a draft. We got meaty pizza goodness and cold Coca Colas or Sweet Tea waiting for hardworking staff. Come on," he motioned her over. "That means you from now on. Dinner is one of the perks of being a member of Barracuda Bail Bonds."

"Here, here!" chorused Pansy and Rose Marie.

Pim trotted ahead, sniffing the air, his tail high. Nessa smiled and closed the door.

Outside, the shadows deepened and the stars winked on. Fat gray clouds moved slowly across the open sea to hover just offshore. On the sidewalk in front of Barracuda Bail Bonds, a tiny spider web of shadows blossomed, slowly circling a drop of dried blood.

To be continued in Girl's Guide to voodoo Bounty Hunting 2: Shifty Business

Scroll down for a preview of Nessa and Pim's next adventure in bounty hunting!

Sneak Preview

Girls Guide to Voodoo Bounty Hunting
Book 2: Shifty Business
By Eden Crowne

Copyright 2021 by Eden Crowne. All rights reserved

CHAPTER ONE

Nessa hit the brakes on her scooter, grinding to a stop on the unpaved driveway in a spray of gravel. Pim meowed in protest at being thrown against the metal bars of the basket. She braced herself with both feet before flipping open the lock on the lid.

The Victorian mansion at the end of the road looked like the Psycho house on the Universal Studios backlot tour. To complete that image, a young woman sat on the porch steps with a cigarette dangling from her lips, a bottle of beer in one hand, and a double-gauge shotgun resting across her lap.

The girl was long-legged and lanky, inky black skin and hair in an old-school Afro. Nessa immediately thought of her boss, Roman Barracuda, and his Cool and the Gang seventies-celebration style. She wore cut-offs, a faded pearl button red plaid cowboy shirt, and lace-up leather work boots.

A row of black stitches made a frown line over her left eyebrow, bruises on her cheek were turning yellow, and her lower lip was split and scabbed.

"Did you bring the bottle?" she asked around the cigarette.

Nessa swallowed, her throat dry, watching the shotgun.

"The bottle," the girl repeated. "Did you bring it?"

Shifting her backpack around to the front, Nessa reached in and pulled out a clear glass bottle about eight inches tall with a narrow top and a cork stopper. A braided leather cord was looped around the neck, long enough to make a handle.

She held it up.

The young woman gave a quick nod. "Hold onto it for now."

Pim hopped out of the basket onto the loose gravel. Her Familiar was under an invisibility curse. Unless he transformed into his werecat form, only Nessa and a few other magic users could see him. That list now included her boss at Barracuda Bail Bonds, Roman Barracuda. But since he was also a Voodoo King maybe it was to be expected.

Pim's invisibility was her secret weapon. He could scout and spy unseen.

"Who's your friend?" the girl asked, shifting the shotgun slightly.

'What?' Nessa thought in alarm.

"You can see him?"

The girl gave a quick toss of her head. "No. The gravel shifted in front of the scooter."

Nessa frowned at her Familiar. That had been careless.

The cat bobbed his head and hung his tail in apology stepping silently to the side, not a stone shifting.

"He's Pim. Pim's Cup Whisker's Rampant. My Familiar. Please don't shoot him. Or me." The last part just sort of tumbled out. She hadn't meant to say it out loud.

The girl smiled then winced as it stretched her torn lip. "This isn't for you." She patted the gunstock.

Barracuda's main Skip Tracers were twin sisters Pansie and Rose Marie LaRue. Extraordinarily large red-headed warriors who looked human but most certainly were not. Today they were down south in San Diego and Nessa and Pim were handed the assignment.

"Easy job," Barracuda had said, handing her the paperwork. "Darryl Deschamps Fauvier. Darryl missed his Infernal Court date in Colorado a few weeks ago."

When the real-world police picked Fauvier up in Pasadena on a local assault charge, his prints came up in the system and pinged Barracuda on the Dark Net. The man had run from an Infernal Court date in Colorado. Once he was out of state, her boss explained, it was open season after ten days on Infernal felons no matter who put up the bond.

Infernal Courts for supernaturals worked a lot like judicial courts for humans. And Barracuda Bail Bonds operated much the same as any other office in that business for felons who run afoul of the law. Real-world or supernatural.

"There is someone on-site already, she'll bag him for you. You just transport him to the Infernal Court in Redondo Beach."

"On my scooter?"

Nessa's lack of four-wheeled transportation was a source of friction with Barracuda. She couldn't afford a car. Most of her money, what little she could make, went to tuition at Santa Monica City College or into savings for Long Beach State. She and Pim got around L.A. on her bright orange Suzuki scooter.

"It will be fine. Here." He'd given her the bottle. "You'll need this."

Looking around the front yard, if you could call a massive gravel driveway, stand of acacia, and a patch of dried grass a yard, Nessa didn't see anyone who might be the runaway Darryl.

"Barracuda said you'd have our Skip."

"And I will." She took a long pull on the beer, then gave Nessa a toothy smile. "Very soon."

There was something ominous in the way she said it that made the hair stand up on the back of Nessa's neck. Pim felt it too. He ran back to the scooter, jumped on the seat, and turned a couple of tight nervous circles. Pim wanted them to leave.

Should they go? Nessa was barely one week into the job of Bounty Hunter. The rules of the game were still a mystery. But if she wanted to get paid, and she did, she needed to bring in Darryl. School fees at Santa Monica City College were due in a month. No Skip, no pay.

The girl dropped the cigarette on the porch steps, stubbing it out with her work boot. "Put the scooter around the back. Stay on the porch until I tell you otherwise. Keep the bottle ready."

Not sure what else to do, Nessa followed her instructions. She carefully stepped around the girl and the large gun on her return. Pim didn't need steps. He jumped up through the porch railing. His fur was bristling. Not completely standing on end, but getting close.

"Do you want to talk?" She made a motion toward her backpack. The Speak and Spell was zipped inside.

Pim shook his head.

Cat's vocal cords – even magical cats – are not made for human speech. Pim had six claws on his front paws, the extra one working as an opposable thumb. He could read and write -sort of e- but his paws were too awkward to type on most keyboards.

Pim had been her grandmother's Familiar before coming to Nessa. Grandma' Hattie had hit on the *Speak and Spell* with its chunky keyboard back in the day. Since then, they'd modified the electronic toy until it had as much computing power as a tablet computer.

Nessa always carried the little red machine in her backpack.

Nessa sat in a frayed rattan patio chair to wait for she wasn't sure what. Pim jumped in her lap. The chair sagged and creaked under their weight. Nervously she fingered the amulets on her belt, running her fingers over the charms for wind and rain.

It had taken her and Pim almost two hours to travel across the city from the Bail Bonds office in Compton to Pasadena. She couldn't take the scooter on the freeway. The little machine's top speed was only forty-five miles an hour. Once they'd reached the hills it had been the map-app and many wrong turns before finding the house on an unmarked dirt road. She still wasn't sure how she was going to get this Darryl guy all the way to the Infernal Court in Redondo Beach on the back of her scooter.

"The bastard did this to me," the girl said, startling Nessa. "In case you're wondering. Sucker punched me and I hit my head falling. Knocked me right out. Probably a good thing. He was high and lost interest after a couple of kicks, I guess. I called the cops, pressed charges. It's been about a week. He made bail this morning. The asshole made it very clear he's coming for me."

Vagabonding around the country with Deadbeat Dad, Nessa had seen her share of abusive men. Judging from the girl's tone, Darryl was not going to get in any free kicks this time.

Nessa and Pim sat quietly waiting. Tessa was good at waiting. A childhood spent aiding and abetting her scamming dad had taught her patience. Crickets chirped and locust buzzed in the scraggly acacia tree and the scrub dotting the hillside. It was late afternoon and still hot. Pasadena and the hills were much hotter than the South Bay cities by the seas where Nessa lived.

They heard the truck long before they saw it, roaring up the rough road.

The girl set her beer bottle on the step, the rifle still resting in her arms. She looked totally relaxed. Nessa couldn't say that about herself. Her insides clenched tightly and she wished she'd asked to use the bathroom.

A red pickup sped dangerously along the road, weaving from side to side.

'Drunk or high?' Nessa wondered.

The driver managed to execute a masterful drift turn in the gravel of the driveway, coming to a stop a few yards from where the girl stood.

A man jumped out, yelling before his feet hit the ground. "Desiree! You stupid bitch."

He was a white man, medium-sized with lots of muscle bulging out of a tight white tee-shirt. Thick neck and dirty blond curly hair. That's about all Nessa could take in before he turned to the bed of the truck, still yelling.

The expletives were strung together thick and fast. The basic message between the swear words being: I am going burn your god damn house to the ground with your screaming body in it.

Nice.

They must have been dating. Lust made people do stupid things. That's why she didn't date. Boys were a danger she could not indulge in. Not with a Fallen Angel on her tail.

Darryl pulled up a pair of red metal two-gallon canisters. "You think you can call the cops on me? *Me?*" He was spitting with anger.

Setting the canisters on the ground, he yanked a knife from a sheath across his chest. It was almost a foot long with a serrated edge.

Nessa scooted back in her chair, holding her breath. Pim jumped onto the porch rail, pacing, a growl rumbling in his chest. He began the rippling body movement that singled an imminent shift to werecat mode.

If necessary, Pim could take this guy. As a cat, he was twenty pounds. After transformation, he weighed close to seventy and had the strength to snap bone with a single bite. He could even break a man's neck. The werecat had the uncanny ability to unhinge his jaw like that extinct Tasmanian Wolf. It was the creepiest thing to see. Nessa didn't know if all werecats could do that or not. Pim was the only one she'd ever met.

Darryl stalked over, knife up, his face ugly.

Desiree, that's what he'd called her, did not seem upset at all. She calmly stood, stepped off the porch, shifted the shotgun, and pumped both barrels into his chest.

The bullets blasted a bloody hole big enough to put a man's fist through.

CHAPTER TWO

Darryl was dead where he stood. He didn't even have time to look surprised. His head snapped back and he fell to the ground, sending up a cloud of dust when he landed

Nessa immediately started edging to the side of the porch. She intended to shimmy through the rails, grab her scooter and get them the hell out of there.

Desiree reloaded the gun, saying over her shoulder, "You want to collect for Barracuda, you and that bottle need to stay right here."

Edging closer to the railing, Nessa said, "I think I'm good."

"What? You feel sorry for that son of a bitch? He came here to kill me and burn down my Grandmama's house."

"I get that. But I don't want to end up like him."

The girl was already on the move. Shel put the gun at half-cock and laid it on the bottom step before dragging a bulky green duffel bag out from under the porch.

"Don't be a wuss. Barracuda sent you. I go to church with him. He would have the skin off my back if I touched a hair on your head. And I do not mean that figuratively. Bring your damn self and the bottle down here. Oh, and tell your cat to chill."

Pim was poised to pounce, already transforming and fully visible. He looked at Nessa to say the word. Werecat Pim was a formidable ally. He was also a little crazy and not always in complete control of his claws and teeth.

"Wait," she said making a damping down motion. "Not yet."

Pim gave a low-voiced growl, not liking the situation but he shrugged back into invisibility.

With a skip and a jump, Desiree reached the dead man, dropped the duffel bag, and ran to the bed of the pickup.

This was not the first dead body Nessa had seen. Not like it gets easier but still, not the first and not the worst.

"Come on," the girl shouted over her shoulder. "Time's short!"

"For what?" Nessa shouted back. "That man is in the past tense."

"Not in voodoo he isn't!"

Making a wide circle around the body, Nessa squeaked in surprise and stumbled when a large dog popped up from the bed of the truck.

The girl was fussing with a leash tied to the rack over the truck's back window. Getting it free, she ran back to the duffel. The large dog, as in awfully large, jumped to the ground and galloped behind, wagging its fluffy tail.

"This is Chuck," the girl waved a hand at the dog. "Chuck this is, um, I don't know."

"Nessa. I'm Nessa. And my invisible cat is Pim. Pim likes dogs, so please be nice," she added as Pim happily trotted over to sniff the newcomer. Not that Pim was in any danger. He could handle just about anything on four legs or two.

The dog thrust his nose in the air, then close to the ground. Nessa wasn't sure if he could see Pim but he would smell the feline. Chuck's tail wagged harder as Pim put his nose up to the dog's muzzle. They sniffed each other and Pim rubbed against Chuck's front legs, claiming him.

Pim meowed cheerfully. He liked dogs.

Desiree twisted off the gas caps and emptied the containers over the body. While she did that, Chuck trotted over, lifted a leg, and peed on dead Darryl.

The girl laughed long and loud. "Good boy, Chuck!"

Chuck woofed and wagged his tail. Nessa had the feeling he was more than a dog, in the same way Rose Marie and her sister were more than human.

Desiree got down to magical business. She placed several large red and white squares of material under the head and feet of the dead man. From the duffel, she took out a gallon-sized plastic jug and swiftly made a thick circle of gray ash around the body.

Pins and needles coursed through Nessa's fingers and toes. Oh crap. That was magic and not the nice kind. The ash had to be corpse powder. Great. This magic circle was not for happy puppy and kitten magic. Nope, nope, nope.

The circle wasn't quite complete, she left a small opening in the ash. That meant the girl had more magic to lay down before sealing it.

Next out of the bag was a clear plastic bag of old-fashioned metal keys. She placed them outside the ash circle in a neat row.

Next was a platter holding a hunk of meat, like a roast, covered in plastic wrap.

Chuck licked his lips.

"Not for you, big guy!"

She unwrapped the platter and set the meat outside the circle in front of the keys. This was followed by a bottle full of some brown liquid. Squinting in the failing light, Nessa thought she saw a pirate guy with a cutlass. Rum, maybe?

Opening the bottle, she poured a generous measure into a glass and set those down by the meat.

In front of all the offerings, she placed a rustic cross of branches tied together and on either side of that, two large pillar candles. She lit the candles, then stood back to survey the circle and impromptu altar. Because that's what the food, drink, and etcetera were. An altar.

'To who?' Nessa wondered.

Or what.

The whole process had been accomplished in three or four minutes.

"This girl is not new to magic," she whispered to Pim.

He nodded in agreement.

No blood had been offered yet. Maybe the hunk of meat took the place of that? Or maybe dead Darryl's blood was the offering.

That thought made her stomach lurch. Good thing she hadn't eaten since breakfast.

Nessa must have made some sound since the girl said, "Darryl is going to wake up spiritually very soon. He will try and call Baron Samedi or some other Loa to keep himself from crossing over. Offer his soul for the energy to ride another body, since he is too damaged. We need the Guardian of the Crossroads on our side."

"Who you calling *we* sister?" she said out loud. "I've got my own problems."

The girl didn't answer.

The duffel was looking much flatter now but it held one more surprise. Flares. Two of them.

Nessa began to back up. The girl ignited both and threw them into the circle, immediately closing the ring of ash with a little pop of power. A blink of an eye later and the gasoline exploded.

Pim jumped, turning a somersault in the air and running up onto the porch. Nessa very nearly did the same. Her heart was pounding and her knees felt rubbery.

Chuck seemed unconcerned. He stayed sitting near the girl. Alert but calm, ears swiveling forward and back.

The magic circle contained the flames. The smoke and the smell? Not so much.

Nessa backed up, gagging at the smell of burning flesh.

"Hey," the girl shouted. "Stay close. Have the bottle ready."

The only sound that came out of Nessa's mouth was a choked, "*Gack!*" As she covered her face with her arm. It didn't help.

Desiree spread her hands wide and began to chant in a singsong voice that had goosebumps crawling up and down Nessa's skin. It sounded like French but she wasn't sure. Covering her ears, Nessa tried not to listen. If you were aware of magic, magic could be aware of you.

Pim hissed and stayed on the porch. His back arched, tail stiff, ears flat. He was not a happy cat.

Very quickly a form appeared in front of the little altar. A bent old man. Bearded, leaning on a cane.

Desiree prostrated herself and spoke at length in the same language as the chant.

Nessa lowered her eyes to her feet and scuffed at the gravel. Witnessing magic could sometimes draw you into the spell. Nessa had no desire to be part of this. She had enough ghosts in her life already.

A new smell drifted across the driveway. Cigar smoke. Thick and heady.

Taking a quick glance, she saw someone else appeared, though maybe six or eight feet behind the old man. A tall, skeletal figure. He wore a top hat tilted at a jaunty angle and an old-fashioned frock coat. He had a fat cigar in one hand and was waving it in the air. Most of his body was hidden in a white mist that pooled around his feet as he walked.

At that moment, the charred corpse of Darryl sat up in the circle and screamed.

Bones turning to jelly, Nessa fell in the gravel driveway, her legs splayed out in front of her.

Pim was there in a heartbeat, putting himself between her and the ceremony, already in his werecat form and howling a challenge.

The man in the top hat glanced their way and she looked back. The face came into focus and she desperately wished it hadn't.

ABOUT THE AUTHOR

Eden Crowne is an American author of occult fiction from California. In her other life (and identity) she was an international journalist based in Asia but now writes fiction full-time. She divides her life between Japan and California and her fiction reflects magic from both Eastern and Western sources.

Visit her at: edencrowne.com

Made in United States
Orlando, FL
04 December 2022